W9-BRS-785

By

Sarah Aronson

DISCARD
Library Media Center
NEUQUA VALLEY HIGH SCHOOL
2360 95th STREET
NAPERVILLE, ILLINOIS 60564

A DEBORAH BRODIE BOOK
ROARING BROOK PRESS
New York

Text copyright © 2007 by Sarah Aronson

A Deborah Brodie Book
Published by Roaring Brook Press
Roaring Brook Press is a division of
Holtzbrinck Publishing Holdings Limited Partnership
175 Fifth Avenue, New York, New York 10010
www.roaringbrookpress.com

All rights reserved
Distributed in Canada by H. B. Fenn and Company, Ltd.

Library of Congress Cataloging-in-Publication Data
Aronson, Sarah.
Head case / Sarah Aronson. — 1st ed.
    p.   cm.
"A Deborah Brodie book."
Summary: Seventeen-year-old Frank Marder struggles to deal with
the aftermath of an accident he had while driving drunk that killed two people,
including his girlfriend, and left him paralyzed from the neck down.
ISBN-13: 978-1-59643-214-7
ISBN-10: 1-59643-214-4
[1. Paralysis—Fiction. 2. People with disabilities—Fiction. 3. Rehabilitation—Fiction.
4. Medical care—Fiction. 5. Drunk driving—Fiction. 6. Family problems—Fiction.] I. Title.
PZ7.A74295Hea 2007   [Fic]—dc22   2006101509

1 3 5 7 9 10 8 6 4 2

Roaring Brook Press books are available for special promotions and premiums.
For details, contact: Director of Special Markets, Holtzbrinck Publishers.

Book design by Laurent Linn
Printed in the United States of America
First edition September 2007

For Michael

acknowledgments

Although writing is certainly a solitary process, I did not write this book alone. Many friends and fellow writers helped me along the way. These words will never fully express how much I appreciate their advice, patience, and faith. It is my privilege to thank them here.

To my agent, Barry Goldblatt, for insight, humor, three chances, and a new community of amazing and talented writers. Heartfelt thanks to my editor, Deborah Brodie, for her wise advice, killer suggestions, support, and enthusiasm. I am so honored to be part of the Roaring Brook family.

To the students and faculty of the Vermont College MFA in Writing for Children and Young Adults, especially my four brave and overworked advisors: Kathi Appelt, Jane Resh Thomas, Margaret Bechard, and Tim Wynne-Jones. Kisses to the esteemed members of the Ginger Hair Society. Single malts for all!

To my writing friends, the Upper Valley Writing Group, and everyone who came to the Novel Writing Retreats at Vermont College. Cindy

Faughnan, Kim Marcus, Joette Hayagashima, Ed Briant, Bethany Hegedus, and Jo Knowles: thanks for reading my work over and over again.

Thanks to Kellye Crocker, who, I promise, will be thanking me one of these days. Your friendship and sense of humor got me through—and kept me awake—on many tough nights. Chai-fives to the students and teachers of the UVJC School. Thanks to Deb, Gloria, Bayle, Pam, Becky, Devora, Rebecca, Jeff, Gail, Jill, Rabbi Ed Boraz, Sue, and Lev. To the young men and women who forever touched my soul by letting me help them recover from injuries, I send my humble appreciation and admiration, and hope this book does justice to your mighty spirits and humor in the face of adversity. And special thanks to Tanya Lee Stone, sister by choice, mentor, advisor, and friend. I could fill many pages with all you have taught me about writing, life, and girlhood.

To my family: my parents, Rich and Judy Aronson; my sisters, Miriam and Anne; as well as Brian, Phil, Aaron, and Rachael.

Last, to my children, Rebecca and Elliot: You sacrificed time and vacations. You did your homework without my help. You played in your rooms and gave me space so I could write. And to Michael. Thank you for your confidence, your strength, and for honoring my dream. All of you have given me a safe place from which to venture. I love you! There is no way I could have done this without you.

discharged

Two people are dead. I have to spend the rest of my life in a wheelchair, paralyzed from the neck down.

For the record, I smoked pot twice and I cheated on one exam in ninth grade. I had sex with Meredith, even though I didn't love her.

Justice, to me, was as simple as Newton's third law of motion: for every action, there is an equal and opposite reaction.

Now I know better. Sometimes the reaction is bigger than the action. Sometimes the punishment doesn't fit the crime. Justice is a bullshit concept created by some scholar who never spent one day strapped to a bed in a hospital, unable to move a muscle.

One mistake.

One bad night.

One too many drinks.

You think you know the rules. *Just say no. Wear a helmet when you ride a bike. Buckle up. Study hard. Don't let your friends drive drunk.*

Now look at me.

Mornings suck. In dreams, I walk. I touch myself. I scratch my own ass. In the light of day, I need help to put my glasses on. I move my wheelchair with my chin.

Walk, run, touch, fuck? Never, never, never, and never.

Actually, afternoons and nights suck, too.

"I'm sorry, Frank," Dr. Rockingham said. "But, please, don't lose hope."

"Easy for you to say." Rockingham might have earned an MD and a PhD, but he wasn't a good liar. Science is decades away from figuring out how to fix me.

I'm a head.

My mother disagrees. "You could be dead, like those four kids in Florida." Or the young man in Nevada, the old lady in Tennessee. She lists headlines, bad news, from memory. "Thank God you're alive." Since my accident, she's prayed every morning: first for a full recovery; then for a functioning arm or leg; now it's, *Please, God, let my son accept his body for what it is.*

My father thinks God's a joke. He looks at my useless limbs, my shriveled dick, and walks out for a scotch, single malt. I think about talking to Dad, man to man, head to body. "Go ahead, Dad, pull the plug. Smother me. Anything," but I don't have the nerve. What if I'm wrong? What if my mom is right and God's just waiting for me to prove my faith so he can cure me? Maybe the science is wrong. Maybe I'm missing the big picture.

Chill out, Frank, God here. I just gave you this pill so you believed that you were paralyzed, that you killed Meredith. Get up. Walk. Come see her. She's been waiting for you, right here, all this time.

Really, none of this should be happening. I am seventeen years old.

Someone knocks on the door. "Good morning, men." Cecilia, the nursing assistant, makes a quick soft-shoe beeline past Richard Freeberg's bed to mine. "I changed shifts just so I could be here to see you."

Cecilia grabs my glasses off the bedside table and in one swooping motion, slides them onto my face. The wonderful world of rehab comes into focus. "Thanks, Superwoman."

"No problem, bud." Cecilia, the hero of us crumpled, disfigured gimps and crips, smiles the way she does every morning—like we're all here for some high-class party or award ceremony. Her teeth are about three sizes too big and the left one in the front is chipped. She doesn't care. She smiles all the time—when she comes in, when she cleans me, when she single-handedly gets me out of bed, into my chair. "Sleep good?"

I control my urge to say, "You mean, sleep *well*." Walking Frank loved to point out other people's grammatical problems. Walking Frank had to feel smarter than everyone else.

"So-so, I guess." She puts both hands on my shoulders to straighten me out. Cecilia can't get started until I'm dead center in the bed.

"What's the diff?" I asked her once.

She didn't have much of an answer. "I don't know. Habit, I guess. My mother couldn't keep house to save her skin. I guess I just like things neat."

She shifts my body again and again and one more time,

wedging my nose into her cleavage. She's short, so she's practically on the bed with me. The straps of her pink push-up bra stick out, her T-shirt is crinkly. Her heavy silver cross hits me smack on the chin. "Sorry," she says, tucking it into her shirt, out of sight, and shifting me one last time.

"Nice job, Doctor Love." Makeup cannot camouflage the gigantic hickey on her neck. It's easily the size of a quarter.

Cecilia pretends to smack me across the face. "Don't go there, pal." She steps back from the bed and points the remote control at me like she's going to shoot. "Elevator up," she jokes. "Time for breakfast."

"What's on the menu?"

"Cereal with milk. Last night's fruit cocktail. Toast." She picks up a napkin, and places it under my chin, for no good reason; she'll be undressing me shortly. She feeds me little bites, just the way I like it, and every three or four is ready with the OJ.

The hickey has a little blue spot.

"Oh, Cilia," Freeberg whines, "this bran shit tastes like fuckin cardboard."

She covers her neck with her hand. "That's nice." With Freeberg, it's best to react as little as possible.

After I'm done with my last spoonful, she puts my tray on the counter, picks Freeberg's pants off the floor, and chucks them across the room. "You're a slob, Richard," she says. Her ponytail bobs up and down as she struts past the foot of my bed to snatch my chart. Freeberg just grunts; he's always a bastard after breakfast. She hums while she reads.

"Looks good, Frank." She's holds my chart with one hand, the other is glued to the hickey. Not an easy feat—my chart is as thick as a phone book. She sets it down and shakes out her hand. "Last call, Marder. Anything to report on this fine and most magnificent day?"

"Would you believe I went for a ride with my buddy, Freeberg, and we ate three ice cream sundaes?"

She laughs at my joke—it's part of her job. I've been lying in this bed all night, and we all know it.

I'm a head. I'm a head. I'm a head. I'm a head.

"Ran a marathon, too."

That part falls flat.

Cecilia rubs my head. Her hand is moist, hot and cool at once. "Your mom is signing you out as we speak." She picks a piece of cereal off my face and pops it into my mouth. The flake is soggy; it gets stuck on my tongue. "I really liked taking care of you." Cecilia gives me one more big, toothy smile. She is my friend.

Meredith thought people of the opposite sex couldn't possibly be just friends. Sex and attraction trumped friendship every time. But I'm living proof. Now that my sexuality is null and void, I have a ton of girl friends. Not just techies, like Cecilia. The nurses and the cafeteria girls, too.

"Help me, Cecilia!" Freeberg yells. "Help me, please. I have a cramp."

Cecilia looks at me and rolls her eyes. All three of us know what's coming next.

"No, honest," my roommate says. "Really. Right here. It's real, real bad." She turns around, just in case it is bad, and groans. She doesn't have to tell me that he's pointing to his inner thigh and crotch. Ever since he got his first posttrauma erection, he's been begging everyone to give him a therapeutic hand job—in the name of science, of course.

Call it perv head humor. These are our morning rituals. We eat. We talk. We make up stories. Freeberg says something rude. They take care of us anyway. Every morning since we came to rehab.

For me, that would be one day short of six weeks.

Cecilia pulls the drapes around my bed. "I actually look forward to that stunt," she whispers, and shows me a bottle of vanilla milkshake face cream before slathering it on my forehead, cheeks, and ears. "They were giving samples away at the Saks counter." Cecilia had wanted to be a cosmetologist, not a nursing assistant.

You would think that beauty school should be easier to get into. But Cecilia's makeup is pretty tacky and her hair color is two shades lighter than her skin—definitely not natural.

Her old boyfriend used to hit her. Dr. Love took her to Macaroni Grill. My mother says all things happen for a reason.

Cecilia massages the geography of my remaining functioning sensory sites: my temples, my cheeks, my forehead, and my neck. I wonder if I'll ever get an erection. I wish for one more erection.

"Nervous?" she asks.

"It's been a long time since I've been home."

"Mmm."

"I'm going to have to live on the first floor."

She picks up my right hand and holds it up in the air. I smell my stale pit stink; by some higher ability, she does not even wrinkle her nose.

"The school doesn't care if I don't come back. They say I have enough credits to graduate." Freeberg has no trouble getting it up.

"I hated school," she says. "Especially Math."

Her nails are orange ovals, and there is a rhinestone glued onto each one.

"Your nails look good," I say.

"You mean it?" she asks, putting down my hand. "I did it myself."

"The doctor will love them." I take two deep, forced breaths. Too much talking makes me tired. Cecilia understands and continues working in silence. She shaves my chin, plucks my unibrow and brushes my hair. The complete head treatment.

So I can't get a hard-on. What's the point anyway? I can't feel it, can't see it. Can't use it.

"How about your shaving me today, beautiful?" Freeberg asks. Another ritual.

She looks at me, rolls her eyes, and says what she always says. "DIY, baby cakes." *Do it yourself.* He has arms and chest and even some leg; he can put on his own deodorant, go home and have sex. I can't even masturbate. Why did my cord snap all the way across? Why am I completely paralyzed from the neck down? Why can't I DIY?

"Big day," Cecilia says.

"Really big," I say.

"Really, really big fucking day," Freeberg says. None of us has any real privacy.

Cecilia whips off my clothes to wipe down the deadwood—my

legs and arms. She can see my dick. "You're not sad about leaving, are you? Everyone wants to go home." She rubs me with more lotion and powder. I might as well be at the car wash. "It's going to be so great. In your own bed, in your own house . . ." She really should cover my dick already.

"Enough with the melodrama," Freeberg says. "You're making me cry, Cecilia." He pauses. Footsteps. "Head!" he yells. "You got a visitor."

"Hey." Harry Lassiter, best friend since fifth grade, steps inside the curtain. No *Can I come in?* No *Are you decent?* He considers himself family and, thus, above the knock-before-entering cardinal rule.

When is he going to get a clue? When the curtain's shut, Cecilia's working south of the border.

"How's it going?" he asks.

It takes him a full second to figure out why we're not bringing out the welcome wagon. His face drops like he stepped in dog crap. But he does not move. He stands there and looks at the curtain and sputters, "Oh. Sorry. Geez. I'm sorry. I should have knocked."

Should-a, could-a, would-a.

He rubs his hands on his baggy jeans. Crosses his arms over his chest. Then puts his hands in his pockets. But he does not move.

You'd think he was *paralyzed.*

Cecilia waves a towel in my face, then covers my privates. "Hi, Harry. What's shaking?"

"Can you leave?" I ask him, but no one responds. My voice is too weak. I suck in as much air as my lungs will take. "Can you leave?" Deep breath. "Now?" The last thing I need right now is my best friend staring at my useless body.

Freeberg shouts, "Yeah, get the fuck out! Give the head some privacy."

Harry pulls the lid of his Yankees cap over his forehead. He stuffs his hands back in his pockets. He shuffles his feet.

And the pitch . . .

It's a curve. He steps back and stares at the curtain, but he does not leave.

"Your mom told me you were going home today." The forced enthusiasm makes his voice crack. "She asked me to ride with you in the ambulance."

Cecilia keeps washing me. "That is really nice of you. Isn't it?" She raises her right eyebrow, my cue to lose the bad attitude.

Freeberg shouts again. "Do you not understand the goddamned English language? I said get the fuck away from the head, dork!" I smile—can't help it. I might be a head, but at this moment, I am not a dork.

Cecilia stops working. "Why don't you wait outside until we're done, hon?" She turns her back to me. "I'll call you when the prince, here, is accepting visitors."

Harry obeys. He folds and creases the brim of his hat and finally steps outside the curtain. The whole time, Freeberg chants, "Done, hon, done, hon."

Cecilia leans in and whispers, "That wasn't so smart, Marder. He was being nice. You're going to need him."

Yes, I know the drill. A head needs support. Those so-called

Library Media Center
NEUQUA VALLEY HIGH SCHOOL
2360 95th STREET
NAPERVILLE, ILLINOIS 60564

friends. A head should *never* complain when his privacy is violated. A head should be happy that anybody—any walking human beings—want to visit him, even if they do stare at him like he is the main exhibit in the House of Horrors. "If he can't take it, he doesn't have to stay."

Harry's sneakers squeak as he trips out the door. "Have a nice fall," Freeberg says.

Finally, she pulls out clean pants and a shirt. "You could cut him some slack. He's been here almost every day." No pity party here. She is all contempt. "That's a good friend you just pissed off."

I mumble.

"What did you say?"

"Okay. I know. I'll make it up to him."

"Good." Cecilia dresses my lower half first. "Thank the Lord for Velcro," she says. She straightens the wrinkles out of my shirt and centers my head on the pillow. "I gotta leave you here, bud. Transport's taking you home. They want you in the bed. Losers don't feel like transferring you from the chair." She presses the remote until my head is just where I like it. Before she whips open the curtain, she gives my face a hug and wipes her eyes. "I'll go get Harry. You apologize."

"Yes, ma'am."

"And keep in touch. But don't come back too soon."

"You got it."

"And apologize, Frank. Now." She blows a kiss and disappears.

"You see the shit on that girl's neck?" Freeberg asks. He whistles.

"Yeah," I say, taking a breath, trying hard not to cry. It's hard to breathe and stifle tears. "A six-point-oh on the Richard scale."

Freeberg rustles the blankets, throws his legs over the side of the bed, and transfers all by himself to the candyapple red sports chair at the side of his bed.

"Para stud."

"Crip."

"Gimp."

"Head case." He pops a wheelie and rolls on his back wheels to the bathroom. The therapists have already recruited him for the local wheelchair basketball team.

The doctors and therapists have nothing more to offer me. I am a boring case, a complete injury, right out of a textbook. A curiosity, a nightmare, maybe even a freak show, but not a challenge.

I'm leaving exactly as I arrived.

Some people report that when they are close to death, they see a light beckoning to them. A bright, warm glow urges them to follow, come, seek out your ultimate destination. They also feel the pull of loved ones telling them to live, fight, come back. Your time has not yet come.

I didn't see a light. Loved ones did not urge me back. No voices, no music.

I felt nothing. I floated in the most peaceful place in the universe.

I felt nothing. I was alone.

I felt nothing, or maybe it's more accurate to say I felt the absence of everything.

I know the car skidded twenty-five feet before we hit the old man and the tree, before Meredith and I went flying into the window, but that's because the *Mooretown Valley News* covered my story for two weeks running. It was the biggest tragedy in our town's history. In Boston, we would not have caused a ripple. But this was Mooretown. The famed George Washington High. I was the local boy done wrong. Sidebars on national statistics. Testimonies by friends and relatives. They covered it all.

Harry saved every article in a big white envelope.

For the record, it took three paramedics to get me out of the car and get me here in two pieces—ha-ha—although one report said that four people worked for two hours to get me out. "He was conscious the whole time," the EMT driver said. "He told us some jokes. How many people with ADD does it take to change a lightbulb?"

The doctor said, "Everybody laughed. (The answer, *Who wants to go ride bikes?* is on his Web site.) We thought it was a good sign."

The nurse added, "When Frank made that joke, we were sure we were going to save his life. We were confident that we were going to see some magic."

Magic, my ass.

Check out *www.Quadkingonthenet.com*. Post your favorite Meredith story, or read Betsy Sinclair's essay, "My Narrow Escape: I Was Frank Marder's Girlfriend." Read a diary of my medical status or the *Union Leader*'s editorial about "the epidemic of drunk drivers." You can ask questions about spinal cord injury and drunk driving, but nobody does. Or double click on the most popular link: *Vote Now!* Do you think Frank Marder's punishment was adequate?

So far: forty people think I should be in jail. Four think the judge could have been more creative with my sentence. Only two think I've been punished adequately, and one of them is Harry. The other is probably my mother, so that doesn't count either.

My father thinks the Steins paid for the site. They're out for blood. For weeks, they were on the radio, TV, and Internet, memorializing Meredith, begging first the town, then the judge, then the state to do something *substantive*. "Indecent," my mother said. "Media hogs. Taking advantage of their tragedy that way."

I disagreed.

When my parents were hearing the good news, the Steins

were burying Meredith. When my parents were learning about wheelchairs, Meredith's parents were comforting the wife of the old man who never saw me coming. Eenie, meanie, miney, mo—none of us were winners.

Our pictures have been in many papers. Every time, they use our yearbook pictures, the ones we had taken last summer. Hers was black and white, a profile. She's almost smiling. Her hair falls loosely around her face. Mine was more casual. I wore my Sox shirt.

My parents have even been in *The Globe*, toward the back of the first section.

My dad looks solemn in his paisley tie; my mother's eyes and nose are shielded by a low-brimmed hat. Harry, of course, showed me the clipping. "They interviewed me, but they didn't use my name." He points to a paragraph deep in the article. *Marder's friends insist that he was not a chronic drinker. "If anyone was a risk taker, it was Meredith Stein," a source close to both families said.*

"A source close to both families?"

"It's just newspeak."

"Well, don't do it again. Don't badmouth Meredith."

Harry looked confused. "I was just—"

"Do you understand?"

Harry looked away. "The Steins have been on the radio every day this week. They are demanding that the state change the legislation," but he never said how. "They're making you sound like you were a disaster waiting to happen." He left the picture on my bedside table.

The day that picture was taken, the doctors screwed a halo

into my skull to hold my neck in place for the surgery. They ordered test after test after test. But they never got past the same tired questions: "Do you feel this? Frank, do you feel this? Can you move your toe? Your leg? Your hand?"

"How about now?" I wasn't prepared.

"Now?" I just needed time.

"Frank. How about now?"

The answer was no. No. *I don't feel anything.*

The looks were all the same. You know what I mean, the double takes that say loud and clear, *I feel sorry for you,* or *I'm so happy I'm not you.* My favorite is the quick hand to the crotch— one, two, three, *all there,* and a smile. *Thank God, mine still works.*

Still, I couldn't help hoping. "Frank, you have some work to do." The doctors descended upon me in groups of four and five. They had me laid out on this big rolling bed, rolling, rolling, rolling, tilting to the left then right, left then right, over and over again. Machines, light, people, light. They had to strap me in so I wouldn't fall off the ride. "Okay, Frank? How does that sound?"

I said, "Great. Let's do some work."

Thumbs up. I knew how to answer the questions.

Then nothing. The docs made a huddle just out of sight. They talked in low voices. "Frank this. Frank that." I couldn't hear them. The younger ones talked in spurts. High voices. Questions. They looked sad and scared and embarrassed.

I thought they didn't hear me. "Great," I said. "I'm ready to work."

Thumbs up.

When I smiled, they all burst into laughter too quickly. I said,

"I thought we were working. Didn't you tell me you wanted me to work?"

All they did was talk.

"You okay, Frank? How do you feel?"

"You feel this, Frank? How about this?"

"Frank, concentrate. I am moving your foot. Can you tell?"

They had to be joking. They weren't touching me. How about that work, doctor?

"Frank, tell me where I'm touching you."

"Frank, I'm going to prick you with a pin. Can you feel it?"

"Frank, can you move your arm? Your fingers? Your toes? Anything?"

I said, "You're starting to freak me out. What did you give me? I don't feel anything at all."

Hour after hour, or minute after minute, doctors kept bugging me. Same questions. Same answers. I silently made bargains with myself. *I will study harder. I will be nicer to my parents. I will count to ten and my legs will wake up, and my hands will work. I will be able to reach up and hug my mother. I will be honest with Meredith.* I didn't know she was dead.

Day after day, they rolled me, poked me, lifted me, and tested me. They asked me a million questions, all the same. *Frank, can you feel this?* Their voices grew louder, desperate. FRANK, CAN YOU FEEL THIS? All the time, I waited for an assignment, something I could do, a shred of hope, some good news. Some work to do.

I waited. One week. Two weeks. Still, no work. They moved me from the ICU to rehab. Did I miss something?

Hello. If anyone is listening, I'm still waiting.

A light is always on. A machine is always beeping. They can hear us through the intercom.

Even today, moving day, a constant stream of visitors flows in and out of the room. After Cecilia leaves, the black guy who takes your vitals comes. Then it's the urine girl. She has a big, round butt, and she's not afraid to shake it in Freeberg's face. After that, the chaplain shows up to pray with me. That gets Freeberg moving. He rustles around, bed to chair, chair to bed.

"Push through your wrists and lift your ass *off* the bed," I remind him. Heads can hear every move they can't make.

The chaplain, Father Joe, sits in the chair next to my bed. He reads a passage I don't understand. It doesn't matter—it's always the same refrain. Find God. Love God. Believe in God.

He crosses my dead body. "You have to believe. You have to trust that He has a plan."

He can't possibly expect me to buy that line.

Still, I never balk over a blessing. If there was a rabbi in the house, I'd let him in, too.

"Is the Padre history?" Freeberg asks from the door, even though he can see I'm alone. He rolls around the room, popping wheelies, flexing his biceps, using all and every one of his neurologically intact muscles. "I can't wait to blow this taco stand." He's leaving tomorrow, and already, he's got big plans. "It's going to be fucking awesome. Badass Jack's bringing the pickup truck and we're going straight to the city. You gotta come meet the guys. Hang out. Two dollar drafts," he says. "Hookers."

Richard Freeberg is a high school dropout, a dreg, a punk. He has a prison record that cannot be expunged. The only thing he's really good at is "fuck speak." He can use the word *fuck* in multiple grammatical derivatives.

My first day in rehab, he rolled up to me and asked, "What the fuck is your problem? You never seen a fuckin para-pa-legi-ac before?" He jabbed me in my dead shoulder. "You a head injury, too? Don't tell me they put me with a fuckin zombie."

"I am not a zombie," I said. "I just don't feel like talking." At least, not to someone like him. My parents came in with a box of cards to hang on the wall.

"Hey, there," he said. My father nodded.

My mother sensed no danger and cornered him for a little game of twenty questions.

"What's your name? How were you injured? How long have you been in treatment? Did you know that most spinal cord injuries happen to males between the age of eighteen and twenty-two?"

"You don't say." Freeberg balanced and spun on his back wheels until my mother clapped.

When she turned her back, he wagged his tongue.

"You know," she said, "three years ago, Channel Thirty-nine did a weeklong series on traumatic injuries. I taped it. If you like, I'll bring it in."

"Three years ago?"

"Yes. It was very interesting."

"Rosemary, give me a hand," my father said, pulling her to my side of the room, as if her virtue were at stake. "I'm sure Frank's roommate—"

"Freeberg. Richard. But you can call me—"

My father turned his back. "I'm sure Richard has plenty of things to do."

When they left, Freeberg called me a fuckin snob. "Your mom's nice. How come she stays with that asshole?"

I wanted to punch him.

If I had arms.

But by my third day, the sex talk was better than my mother's audiobooks, Harry's score sheets, or my father's cold shoulder. By the end of the week, I almost admired the three tattoos, especially the one "down there," right above his pubes. "See here?" he said. "These are Rosey's lips. Rosey Johansen." He grabbed his crotch. "Oh baby, she was hot! She was thirty-two when I was sixteen, and she taught me everything I know."

Today he won't stop talking about the potential sex he can get from looking pathetic. "Seriously, you should come out with us. One look at that chair, and we'll all get lucky."

"I thought you made plans with that hottie nurse, Zoe." Freeberg looks like he doesn't know what I'm talking about. He talks a good game, but sometimes he lies.

Zoe used to be our night nurse until she got caught doing Freeberg in the patient lounge after hours. At least, that's what he says.

But maybe she just got transferred to another floor. Or she turned him down. I can't imagine choosing beer over a girl with double-D breasts that you can see through a bra, a T-shirt, and a hospital-issue top, but then again, I'm not Freeberg. He has the rest of his life to have sex.

Freeberg reconsiders. "Hell, maybe I should call old Zoe. You know, I bet she could find someone to fuckin sit on your face. What do you say, Frank? You know, like, it's better than nothing."

She walks into my room, completely naked. She climbs onto my bed, wrapping her legs around my dead body so she can kiss me. Her long brown hair tickles my face. Her hair is so soft, and I open my mouth, alive and intact, hard as a rock. The fantasy is perfect until she looks at me. Meredith. She covers herself and vanishes. *Poof!* No hookers, no friends, no parties in the back of the truck.

I don't deserve another chance.

I should tell Freeberg, no, no thanks, sorry, buddy. I'm going to go home to my room and never open the door. Die.

But instead, I play along. "Sure, man, that would be fucking awesome," the way he would, but instead of laughing, he says, "Uh-oh." It must be Harry, still sulking, back for his apology.

I wait for the shuffle steps, the Yankees score sheet, some new joke about dumb blondes. A Coke. Gossip from school. Took him long enough.

My mother's cheeks are flushed, but her face is dead and expressionless. She gathers the family pictures off my bulletin board and the stack of cards out of the drawer. "It's cold and gray. We're expecting a drizzle," she says. Right after the accident, I caught her checking me out below the waist. She stared at my legs and began to pray, but the power of her faith couldn't do anything more than modern medicine could.

She wraps the photos in bubble wrap and takes out a rubber band to keep the cards organized.

"We don't have to save them," I say.

She finishes the job, her shoulders slumped. Freeberg shoots an extra rubber band across the room. "Last night, we thought we might get snow," she says, "but we didn't. Not even a frost. The grass looks dead." Like me, like us. Looks dead, but is alive. How appropriate.

Freeberg scribbles his name and phone number on a hospital brochure. "Call me," he says, stuffing it into my bag. He pops a wheelie and spins around. Show off. "If I don't hear from you, I'm coming to get you."

"Great. I'll give you a call ASAP." My mother doesn't smile. She thinks we're sincere, but she's wrong. Freeberg won't come anywhere near our neighborhood. We will never see this guy again.

She sidesteps around him, grabs my bags, and nearly runs smack into the woman who picks up the trays. "I'll be back soon," she says, squeezing past the tall stack of empty plates and cups. Freeberg rolls after the cart, panting like a dog, but stops at the door and settles back on his tires. He blows her a loud and piercing kiss, then cracks up. "She just flipped me the bird."

People call Freeberg "the Cat." As in lucky. Nine lives.

When Freeberg was three, he crossed a highway in his diaper. When he was eleven, he stole a motorcycle and drove it five miles. At thirteen, he got so drunk his stomach had to be pumped. And two years ago, he broke both his legs when he fell off a ladder, trying to visit his girlfriend at three a.m.

Freeberg broke his back when, drunk as a skunk, he jumped into a swimming pool—a perfect cannonball. The only problem was that the owners of the pool had recently drained it. Ouch.

And even then, he didn't break it all the way. He has enough control of his quads to walk to the bathroom with crutches and braces.

My parents can't even look at him.

When I broke my neck, I snapped the cord all the way through.

Cecilia comes back in with one hand behind her back and a big foil balloon floating above and behind her. She must not realize we can see it. "Surprise." She extends her arms to my face. After a momentary lag, the balloon follows. She ties it to my chair. "It was the only one they had," she says. She wiggles past Freeberg, who pinches her ass.

The balloon says, *Get Well Soon.*

Freeberg bats the balloon. "You want to suck it?" he asks.

When I was a kid, I loved sucking helium. The summer between seventh and eighth grade, Harry and I mowed four lawns in one day just so we could buy the deluxe bouquet. Sixteen balloons. We couldn't wait.

In my room, sweaty and tired, we took turns, sucking in the helium and laughing like crazy, until my dad walked in. "What are you two doing?" he yelled. "Don't you have any respect for your bodies?"

Ironic. But those were the years of "treat your body like a temple"—my father worked out every morning, didn't eat eggs or red meat or bacon. That day, he yanked the balloon carcasses out of our hands, dumped them in the garbage, and grounded me for a week. I didn't care. Sucking gas is one of those rights of passage, like your first bike, your first home run, your first kiss, your first time.

Meredith was my first.

When she was happy, her smile made me feel strong. Physical. Before her, the biggest risk I took was swinging at a three-and-two pitch with two outs in the inning. Before her, I'd only kissed girls. Twice.

Cecilia's pink-and-green balloon bobs up and down, like it's laughing at a good joke. Freeberg bats it one last time.

"No." I am not going to suck the helium. I am not going to meet the guys. My life is over.

I stare at my wheelchair at the side of my bed. The doctor says that the wheelchair is the key to independence, but my mother has to put me in it first. What if she can't? What if they decide it is not worth the trouble to take care of me?

What happens then, Doctor? What happens then?

Freeberg is leaving for therapy as my mother walks into the room. "It was nice meeting you, Richard." She holds out her hand, and they shake. "Take care."

She is wearing clothes she hasn't put on in years, clothes she hasn't worn since my parents worked in an office together, when I am sure they still loved each other. "Where's Harry?" she asks. "He said he'd meet us here."

Freeberg feigns dismay. "You mean your friend? The one with the pockmarks all over his face? The baggy jeans? That friend? Shit, I had no idea . . ."

"Frank? What happened?" Mom keeps her nose above and beyond Freeberg. "Where's Harry? You didn't have an argument, did you?"

"See you in the fast lane," Freeberg says, rolling out the door.

I wait for the latest installment of "Richard's crude ways," but Mom is distracted. For my last day in the hospital, she bites her tongue and stares at the chair. Or maybe, she's worried about Harry.

"I should check at the desk or the cafeteria."

Nobody moves. Certainly not me.

"We could call him. He can come back. It's not too late. Plenty of time." She clutches her notebook, the one Dad bought her for their anniversary, the one she had never used until she had to organize her questions.

What if his skin looks red? What if he has a coughing fit? What if I can't get him out of bed?

Not all her questions. Not *What if I can't do it?* The nurses and doctors never answer that one. Never the big ones, like *What if I don't like taking care of my son? Is there a place he can go?* And, of course, never *How did I end up with a paralyzed son and a cheating husband?*

She sits on the side of my bed. "I'll call Harry." She dials, hangs up, dials, hangs up. The line is busy. "I'll try one more time."

"Maybe he took the phone off the hook."

She tries three more times.

"Busy?"

She tries not to cry. Digs through her purse for the travel-size Bible. We have bigger problems.

"Help us, O Heavenly Father. My son needs your help. He needs your strength and wisdom." She prays over me, like it will make a difference. "Help him on this very important day in his life. Give him the strength he needs."

If I had died, my family could grieve. They could rejoice and remember the person I was. Move on.

"Amen." She closes her Bible and rests her head on my chest. Her face is so close to mine, I can see her pores and her smeared makeup, the places where she wiped away old tears.

It's hard to breathe against the weight of her head. She could kill me this way. If she pressed a little harder . . .

"Mom, sit up." I cough. "Mom. I can't breathe." She bolts upright, and my breath returns.

"I couldn't sleep a wink last night," she says, attempting to smooth out my hair. My mother's not a hugger, not like Harry's mom. She needs her space.

My parents sleep in two beds pushed together. They keep a little space, a crack of air between them, so that they don't have to touch. The crack grows maybe twice a year, when he's cheating. She stopped touching me when I grew taller than my father, when she knew that I looked at girls and women.

Now she will have to touch me all the time. She'll have to wash me and stretch me and get me up. She'll have to look at me naked. She'll have to shave and powder me.

Her breath is hot and sweet on my face. She dials Harry's number one more time. She opens the book and squeezes it shut. Open and shut. Open and shut. "Doctor Rockingham should be here any minute. One more conference and we're free and clear." She pats my head. "How do you feel?"

Asking a head how he feels is about as stupid as telling a blind man to look. But able-bodied people—bodies—they can't seem to remember that. They make the same mistake every day: *Hi, Frank. How does that feel—oops.* Even in the hospital, they say it: *feel—oops.* They put on these big clown-face smiles, like I am not just paralyzed, I am deaf or stupid. Sometimes they catch themselves. *Hey, Frank, how do you—yeah. Sorry.*

My mother says it again. "How do you feel?" She does not seem to understand that this idiom, this truly meaningless question, is now a bitter slap in the face. But, actually, I should give her some slack. At least she is trying to make some conversation with me.

Someone knocks on the door and my mother stands up, like we were just caught making out. "Hello, Doctor Rockingham, sir," she says, straightening her skirt, trying to smile through tears. My mother is very impressed with Dr. Rockingham, aka Drock.

"Hello, Rosemary. Hello, Frank." For my last day, our final meeting, he is alone. No gaggle of overworked, sleep-deprived residents to listen to his wisdom today.

I'll almost miss his routine. "This, students, is Frank Marder, a complete C4-5. Can anyone tell me what that means?" They stutter and whisper, like I don't know the truth. "And here's Mr. Freeberg, an incomplete L4, the virtual lottery winner of spinal-cord injuries. Check out the difference between these two young men. Hey, Frank, how do you—"

Just because we can't walk, doesn't mean we are morons. When he comes back after rounds to flirt with sexy Stacey, my physical therapist, he slips the gold wedding band into the lab coat pocket. Freeberg cuts him slack. He forgives anybody anything if they're trying to get a piece of ass. Just don't ask him how he's feeling.

Drock's pathetic. He gives my mother a short, sterile embrace. I get a quick flick of the wrist. "Frank, you must be feeling great today."

Drock is a little doctor, a short, thin man with small hands. He never sits down. Yesterday, Cecilia told me that he has a bald spot in the center of his skull. In the middle of the shiny circle, he sports a large mole, the shape of Oklahoma.

At the head of my bed, he and my mom look down at me. I am still, a breathing corpse.

"Going home. Now that's great news." His voice cracks; he coughs to cover it up, but we both know he sounds nervous.

"Sorry I'm late," my father says, rushing in the door. He towers over Drock. "I had—"

"A meeting?" my mother asks.

Dad straightens his tie.

Drock directs the attention back to me. "You must be thrilled to be going home. We're so happy for you, Frank, so very happy. You've made such progress."

"Progress?" I ask. "Really?"

My father starts rubbing his hands, like he's trying to set them on fire.

"Oh, yes, your skin looks great and you're tolerating . . . let me see"—he checks the chart, but clearly can't find what he's looking for—"hours of time in the chair." He wipes his forehead and shoots Mom a knowing glance. Uh-oh. When there's good news, there's the other kind, too.

"Sadly, though, the van, the new van"—the van they have been talking to my parents about, the van with all the fancy adaptations—"is not quite ready." Drock looks at the wall above my head. There is a nick on the cleft of his chin. "It's just a matter of days, maybe a week or two. The van," he tells the lovely picture of flowers and daisies. "But for now . . . for now, Frank, my man, I feel that it's best that you go home. If you need to get out of the house, there are a number of taxi services you can call." He gives my mother a yellow card. "But the important thing is to start your life today."

The doctor flinches when my father's cell phone rings. "The office," he says, heading for the door.

"Why can't I stay until the van is ready?" Bad question. Drock looks away. *Hey Drock, have you heard the one about the quad and the lying doctor?*

He is ultimately saved by the bell—Stacey appears from outside my visual range to stand next to her man and my mom, a virtual trifecta of smiles. "Hi, Frank." She turns to my mom. "Sorry I'm late." She smiles at me. "Are you psyched to go home?" Her hair is pulled back in a big red headband, a little like Minnie Mouse's. I try to imagine what her words would sound like in a higher octave. "I am so optimistic for you, Frank! Going home will be a total morale booster."

Do they think I'm an idiot? What would be good for my morale is to get up off this fucking slab and walk out of here, not ride, dependent, no feeling, no nothing, no nothing ever again.

Freeberg sails by in his high-tech Quickie. Red. Fast. Built for the basketball court. He pops a wheelie and rests on his back tires, while he scrambles through his bedside table, looking for something. My mother is visibly uncomfortable in the presence of such an independent crip. "Is my car ready?" he asks. Freeberg thinks he's getting a special car with hand controls.

Drock shakes his head. "These things take time, Richard."

Freeberg peels out, and my father reappears, hands now deep in pockets. Drock pulls my parents aside and hands them a packet of papers. They go over schedules and visits to the hospital. They take a few steps away. I hear: school, class, health, and friends. Adjustment, routine.

Health class, tenth grade. Ms. Markham, the new, young teacher, spoke to us with careful diction and a Southern twang. "What disability scares you most?" We sat there, hands folded. We hated when teachers played with our heads.

But we liked Ms. Markham. She was wearing her perky red-

and-white checked dress with the low neck, too low for high school boys to care about the words she was saying.

"Duh . . . retardation," someone said, and everyone laughed, *haw, haw, haw,* like we were the very retards he was referring to. None of us had to worry about disability. We were students. We lived in a suburb with clean streets and pine trees. Our parents had college educations.

Ms. Markham frowned, and raised her hand to regain some control, but all that did was shift her dress slightly to the right, giving me and Harry a nice shot of pink lace and curve.

Harry showed his appreciation by giving her the kind of answer she was looking for. "Paralysis," he said over the remaining spatter of chuckles. "I would rather be dead than paralyzed." The guy in front of me flinched; Harry shook out his legs. Someone else burped.

Hindsight is a head's biggest tease.

My father hands Drock a business card. "If you ever want to double your pension . . ."

"I'll let you know." Drock shakes their hands. For me, he makes his token gesture—not the finger, but not a full wave, before heading for the door. "You've done a great job, Frank."

Mom sits on the edge of my wheelchair and picks the remains of her nail polish.

Dad calls the office. "Yep, we're taking him home today. Thanks, Clarissa. Yes. Yes. Maybe tomorrow."

"Clarissa?"

"The new secretary."

The transport team interrupts the possibility of public accusation. Two scrawny guys—neither of them look strong enough to transfer me. "Good morning, Mr. and Mrs. Marder. How's our guy, Frank, doing today?" The shorter one needs a shower.

"Nice balloon." The clean one punches the smiley face, while the smelly one checks the brake. "You psyched to get out of here?"

Yes. Frank is very excited to leave the hospital. So please do not ruin this perfectly lovely day by doing anything rash or premature. Do not bend him too far; shift him, but do not drag him. Hold the sheets, not him.

"This will only take a minute, Frank. You know the drill." They grab fistfuls of my sheets.

"Frank, we're going to transfer you to the gurney. On three. Okay, Frank?"

What if I say no?

"Are you ready? One. Two."

No. No. You can't. I do not give you permission yet. You have to wait for me.

"Three . . ."

This is my body. My life.

"Lift."

I hear the weight of my body, see the strain on their faces. The smile of success. They tuck in the sheet and strap me down. They talk like I'm not here.

"Man, did you see that new admit?"

"Yeah! Holy shit, the guy must weigh three hundred pounds. I can't believe he's on my service."

They roll me out the door into an elevator, down halls with long fluorescent lights, until we are at the front door.

"Here you are!"

"Here we are," my mother murmurs.

The doors open automatically. The transport guys shoot the shit with the security guard. The light hits my face for the first time in weeks.

The sky is not gray; it is almost white, filled with clouds. I squint to look up. Dad meets us at the door. I try to suck a whole mouthful of fresh air into my lungs. It is one of the few willful acts I can perform.

My mother takes my father's elbow. She is holding Cecilia's balloon.

"Let it go," I say.

My mother begins to protest. "It's a gift. From Cecilia. You don't want to . . ." Her voice trails off.

"Let it go," I repeat. She does. I don't watch it fly away, but I know it does.

For Christmas, my father likes to give me tools. When I was eleven, it was a screwdriver. Then a wrench. At thirteen, a hammer. We made things: birdfeeders, bookshelves, and once, a small table. He said, "This is what men are supposed to do together. We make things with our hands." We cleaned the tools and stored them in a red box in the garage. We'd go back to the house, our manly hands scraped and sore.

When I was fifteen, he gave me the prize I had been hoping for: an axe. We raced to the shed and sharpened the blade. "I bought us some wood," he said. "Your mother loves sitting by the fire." I threw off my coat.

In silence, we worked. Chopping and stacking until we had made two large piles of split logs, enough for a month's worth of New England's dankest nights. My chest ached. He draped his arm on my shoulder. "We men have to depend on one another."

We men.

The transport team talks trash. My parents flank the gurney. Dad stands still, looking at the circle drive, waiting for the ambulance. He has been talking into his cell phone since we left Drock. "Trust me," he says. "This is money in the bank." He waves his hands in the air, talking into the headset, comparing money markets, stocks and bonds. "Depend on me," he says.

This is what men are supposed to do.

My mother touches my head, as if to say yes, this is hard, standing here, waiting. Her nails have lost their color, so she pills the fringe of her scarf.

When the ambulance pulls up to the curb, my father says good-bye, and my mother walks in front of me to take her place at his side. "Here we go," he says. He stands straight, like a soldier. She leans on him. Today, she can.

My mother won't stop talking, talking, talking, talking in that singsong *hey how ya doing, Frank, I love you, Frankie* **voice, like I am a baby and nothing is wrong.** First they load me, then the chair, then my parents. "Don't worry, Frankie, you're going to be just fine." My mother uses her public voice. She is trying to hold it together in front of the young men.

My ears hurt.

She takes a tissue from her purse, brings it to her nose, and blows. Such a simple action; she does it with such ease. Tissue, nose, blow, tissue, nose blow—she does it over and over again. Tissue, nose, blow. She is going to use the whole packet of tissues.

She's scared. I'm scared. We're all scared. We are all one big conjugation of scared. We haven't even pulled out of the hospital parking lot.

She blows her nose again. Torture.

In the back of the ambulance, the light is bright. The life-saving equipment is marked and labeled, ready for action. My mother slumps in her seat, until her face is close to mine. Her long hair lingers on my face and tickles my nose. It smells like roses—fake roses. It makes me want to sneeze, but I'll never turn down human-to-human contact. She sighs very quietly.

"For God's sake, Rosemary, don't cry," my father says. He reaches over me and takes her hand. He holds her hand, like it is precious, squeezing it over and over again above me.

She holds back the tears but pushes away his hand. "I never realized how much equipment there is in an ambulance."

He says nothing more. Nothing to her, nothing to me, nothing to the boys who drive this bus. We never talk. Maybe we have an understanding, but I don't know what that understanding means now. I want to yell. My father is not a perfect man. But he is my father, and he needs to help my mother now.

They shift out of my frame of reference. *Snap*. The buff technician steps up and pulls some straps over my body. Maybe too tight, maybe just right. I don't know. I am cargo, not a man.

Click.

I bet that's just what a jail cell sounds like. *Snap, click. Click, snap.* Good-bye. Go to jail.

Snap.

Click.

"Here we go, buddy," the driver says, revving up the engine. "Next stop, home." Hospital workers love calling crips like me "buddy." They must get told during orientation that this makes us feel comfortable, or maybe it is so they don't have to remember our names. Since I got hurt, I've been "buddy," "pal," "guy," and "big man." The list goes on. Cecilia always called me Frank. Zoe called me Frog. My mom liked her. So did my Dad. Zoe has a great body; I saw him look twice.

We pull out of the driveway and roll over the speed bump. The ambulance rattles, and my mother makes a little shrieking noise. "Could you drive a little slower?"

"Don't worry," the driver says, "we won't break any laws today."

"Well, that's a relief," my father says. He's joking.

My mother never jokes. "Yesterday, on the six o'clock news, Dana Renaldi reported that there were more accidents in the past three months than there had been in the last year."

"Is that so?" one of the guys asks.

"It is. And more fatalities than any three-month period in the last four."

"Okay there, buddy?" my father asks. Yeah, he doesn't use my name, either.

"Yeah," I say, as loud as my supine lungs will let me. I'm sick of being on my back. I hope that one of them will get me into the chair ASAP. We make our way over a second speed bump, and this time, my head jiggles, like the oxygen tank and the first aid kit that are bolted to the wall. They don't roll off and neither do I. We are heavy, inanimate objects. My head is, in many ways, a lot like an oxygen tank.

For some reason, that is reassuring.

home: day one

The house is the same, but different. The green leather couch and the brown recliner are back against the wall, and the coffee table is stuffed in a corner. The chairs do not bring people together. My mother's triple-pile carpet is gone. In its place is space—smooth floor without friction. I sit in my chair in the middle of the room where the EMTs left me. Like a centerpiece.

Mom flops on the couch. "What do you think?" Her lip quivers.

"It's okay." Liar.

I watch my mother try to get up. But she flops back down, not completely unlike Freeberg, when he doesn't shift his weight all the way over his feet. "I'm so happy you're finally home." She's a liar, too.

I sit and wait for her to move.

She slides out of her shoes and wiggles her toes. When she closes her eyes, I wonder if she dreams she is someone else's mother.

I can't be the same child she's been doting on for the past seventeen years.

When other kids ran off to the playground, I clung to her skirt. She would walk me to the swings. "You just have to pump your legs," she would say, "just pump, Frank. You can do it."

She did everything I asked. I was cut from the team, so she organized backyard leagues and took me to games. Baseball and football—she cheered for me and bought me the correct jerseys.

When I joined the debate team, she attended every one of our meets. "You made a great argument, Frank. A compelling, first-rate—"

Hey!

Sweat and whiskey are in the room, and my chair starts rolling even though the motor is disengaged. "Protocol, Dad," I say. "You're supposed to ask first."

"Sorry." My father waves his hand to the wall, his empty glass catching the light. "Look," he says. A fitting order, because what else can I do?

In every free space, he's hung pictures of me jumping, running, swimming, catching. Each picture has a white border and a tasteful, but simple, black frame, the kind you can get at Kmart. It is a cheap but effective shrine of all the things I used to do for fun.

"Nice, Dad." I feel his hand tighten around the base of my skull, then release.

"I need a refill," he says.

"Could you get me a Coke while you're in there?" I really don't enjoy bossing him around.

Dad comes back, puts the Coke and a fresh half-empty glass of scotch on my tray table, and tries to reclaim the moment. "Those were the days," he says, pointing out the picture of me in my vintage Patriots uniform, two sizes too big, with the ball tucked into my pit. He takes the glass off the table and drains it. The remnants of scotch smell like hospital antiseptic and are working their charms. "I remember the day we took that picture. You were so determined."

My father tends to rewrite history. That day, he called me a wuss for not running fast enough to catch the ball.

He points to the baseball shot. My arm is cocked, as if I'm about to hurl the ball. "You had some arm." Some arm. Some average arm. All I see is a boy who couldn't throw hard enough, couldn't catch consistently; an impatient man, a man who wanted to be with someone else. I remember frowns, disappointment, harsh words. *You're wasting my time. You've got hands like a girl.*

Now I've got no hands.

"Could you turn me around?" My voice makes him jump. "Could you help me with that—" He pushes the chair to face the bay window and walks away. One order too many.

The Coke remains, just out of reach.

Outside my window, the big yellow school bus stops, and the able-bodied girls and boys drag backpacks and musical instruments down the steps to the sidewalk.

Clunk, clunk, clunk. They walk like it's a chore. They're tired. It's a hassle to move.

As the bus pulls away, three girls stand and talk at the edge of our lawn in the center of my viewing screen. They are small and skinny, bundled in pink and purple. I watch. I can't help it. I can't go anywhere.

One twirls her hair. The second juts out her hip. The third steps onto our grass. She bends over suddenly—the joke must be hilarious.

My throat is so dry. "Mom?" No answer. I take a deep breath and try again. "Mom?" I feel like a freak, watching these girls.

This time she hears. "Just a minute, Frank. I need to look at something." The TV in the kitchen. The up-to-date news of the moment.

I could close my eyes, but I don't.

The twirler steps away to perform a sloppy handstand. She's not very good. She tries two more times, but she can't balance on her hands for more than a moment.

Maybe her friends laugh. Maybe they encourage her. In any case, she tries again, and this time, flips over onto her butt.

Ten, the judges say. Ten, ten, ten. You are beautiful. You can move.

Do it again and again. Try a cartwheel. Or just walk. Walk across the grass. Torment me.

Don't stop moving.

Old Mrs. Houston, our neighbor for the last ten years, limps toward the girls. She's carrying a stack of white bakery boxes and a small bouquet of flowers.

Apology yellow.

It takes her a while to reach the girls. She's got a bum hip. Arthritis. Tells anyone who will listen that she can predict the weather with that hip.

She's says something, then waves at the window.

I smile. She can't tell.

She waves again.

Again.

She can wave all day if she wants to—I'm never going to wave back.

Mom comes in and bangs on the window. "Honestly, I don't have time for this." But it looks to me like she does. She looks happy to walk out the door and take the pies and flowers. She looks happy to stand and talk. The girls grab their bags and run.

Run for your lives! Didn't you know? The quad king is home!

Mrs. Houston waves with her cane in my direction a few more times before limping home. *No. Oh no, Rosemary. I don't want to disturb your family, not on Frank's first day home.*

Does she think I'm contagious or just disgusting? Just because I cannot wave or grab her flowers or even drink this stupid Coke, still sitting on my tray. It used to be so easy. Me, the person, reaches out, grabs the Coke. No problem. Now I need a holder, a wiper, a placer, a cleaner-upper. And don't forget the empty-er of the bladder. "Mom! I'm thirsty."

The straw is floating up, up, up to the top of the can.

The straw pops up and out and sits on the tray.

My lips are dry.

Rage.

"You sit," my mother says. Reflex over reality.

"Do you think you need to remind me?" Reality over humor.

She takes the Coke and puts a newspaper on my tray table. "You shouldn't joke. There was a car bomb in Jerusalem this morning."

She flips on CNN. "Oh my god, would you look at that." Some celebrity is getting divorced. "I thought they were so happy. Didn't they just have a baby?" My mother is addicted to those twenty-four-hour news networks. It all started on September 11. She began to obsess over bad news and petty gossip.

Unlike other mothers, who shielded their children from visual images of disaster, she marked the anniversary by clipping out the photos and displaying them next to our toast and cereal. Over the photo of the burning towers, she wrote, "I love you. Mom."

At dinner, we heard the day's highlights. I like to call it "The Sick and the Dead Report."

"Oh, for god's sake, Rosemary." Dad rolled his eyes every time she got going. She ignored him and launched into her report. Disaster, natural or otherwise, always came first, followed by the local and family highlights: who's divorcing, whose mother had a stroke, and who had to sell their house to pay their bills, as if their bad luck was our fortune. "Rosemary, not again," my father said, night after night, until he decided it was easier to come home after the dinner hour.

The anchor breaks for a commercial, and she scans the channels until she finds coverage of the bombing from the paper. She's glued. "Nineteen people dead. Mothers and children, too."

She watches two cycles of stories. National, international, celebrity, traffic, and weather. A storm is going to hit Boston sometime today. She gets the slant desk from the back room to prop up the paper. "Relax and read. Dinner will be ready soon."

She takes out the garbage. She sets the table. She puts a pile of newspapers in the recycling container. The pile must be very high. Like a mechanical doll, she walks past me, back and forth, again and again, each time with an armful of bags filled with newspapers.

I read the headlines on the front page three times. Car bombs. Car wrecks. Accidents. A famous politician has brain cancer.

"You done with this?" Dad takes my soda, his glass, and a stray plate into the kitchen. Expressionless. His white button-down shirt has newspaper ink on it. He looks like he wants to punch the wall.

"We know you would help if you could," Mom says.

She puts dinner in the oven, then sweeps around me, then sweeps some more. I sit in the living room, no better than a potted plant. I wish I could take out the garbage, do the dishes, set the table, make dinner, take out the newspapers, clean the bathroom, make my bed. I would do it all, without complaining.

Now I can't even turn the page.

If a fly lands on your leg and you can't see it and can't feel it, is it really there? If your best friend waits until the end of your first day home to show up, is he still your best friend? If you yelled at him, but it was while you were in the hospital, and he left without saying shut up or good-bye, and it was really only about the stress and anger and shock and mourning about being a head, do you still have to apologize?

If you can't have, can you still want?

If your wheelchair only rolls at one or even two predetermined speeds, can you still throw a temper tantrum?

Yes. Yes, yes, yes, and yes.

When Harry shows up, he greets my mother first. "The room looks great, Mrs. M. I like it." For a moment, she looks like she believes him. The room doesn't look like a hospital waiting room, space is a wonderful thing, light is best when it sends an uninterrupted shaft to the floor. He steps into the space in front of the bay window and streaks of yellow sun fan out from behind him. "You really have a knack," he says.

My mother gives him another hug. "That's just what I needed to hear." They stand, together, in front of my chair and look at each other in the light. My mother parts his moppy bangs off his face, flattens the creases in his shirt, and wipes the trace of lipstick off his cheek. They look like old friends, reunited after a long separation. Organ music plays in my head. He looks at her with the respect she never got from me.

This has never bothered me before. Harry always pays reverence to my mom. He always compliments her good cooking, the house, her newest acquisition.

But now I wonder: could she love him more than she loves me?

Harry sits. All I can see is the top of his head. "How's it feel to be home?"

"Okay." Now he stands. Too high. I don't like him looking down at me.

"That's good."

In our past life, I couldn't get him to shut up. Dad said he had goddamn diarrhea of the mouth.

He walks across the room and stares at my father's shrine. "Hey, I remember that day. You had a good fastball."

Today, everyone's a liar.

If I apologize, will he smile, take a deep breath, and become good, old, horny-as-hell, motormouthed Harry? Will he sit back and put his feet on the couch the way he used to? I'm sure he has gossip, maybe even actual news to share. There have probably been auditions. He might have even heard from Vassar. I should ask him. Offer to celebrate. If he got in and he didn't tell me, does that mean we aren't friends? If he didn't get in, will I feel better?

The words are stuck somewhere between the *Hey, how's it going* and him trying not to ask *How do you feel?*

I try to break the ice. "Hey, man, we should start planning our trip to Bermuda." It doesn't come out right. Harry stiffens. He goes back to the photos. My words are sad and pathetic and false.

I try again. Lighthearted and casual sounding, even though they're just as delusional. "For spring break. Like we planned."

Harry does not turn away from those pictures. "Yeah, that would be great, if you're feeling up to it."

"Yeah. Okay." This is not lighthearted conversation. I'm a jerk. I know I'm not going to Bermuda. I know he's having a hard time coming up with something to say. But he's just standing on his legs, half looking at the pictures, and all I want to do is not cry. I don't need *him* to feel sorry for myself.

"Cool. It would be great if you could go." Maybe he thinks the accident also made me stupid, like the head injury guys on the rehab floor, the ones who have to wear helmets to cover up where the doctors opened up their brains.

We sound so formal.

There are many things we could talk about. The debate team. Or drama. I can't remember if he is in a play or about to try out for one.

But why should it be easy for him?

I sit and wait.

Harry digs through a bag. "I told everyone you were coming home. They made cards." They always say the same thing: *Get well soon, Frank. I'll visit you, Frank. You're the man, Frank.* He pulls out a thick stack, and I laugh a nervous, oxygen-deprived laugh. We can't throw a ball. We can't even play rummy. My Bermuda comment lingers.

He opens one card after the next, reads them out loud like I'm blind. *Hi Frank, welcome home. Love, Britney. Hi Frank, when are you coming back to school? Love, Miranda. Hey Frank, basketball team sucks. Really miss seeing you on the sidelines. From, Jack Carlson, Mike Bogler, and Tom Stengle.* Harry sounds so earnest, using every one of his drama club lessons.

"That was nice of Tom to send a card," my mother calls from the other room.

Last year, we referred to Mike Bogler as Bulger and I didn't think Carlson knew who I was or even how to write. I don't care about these people.

She puts some cookies on the table for Harry, who grabs two and stuffs them in his mouth. She stands between us and feeds me a morsel. He looks away, like I'm naked again.

"I also printed some of the latest comments from *www.Quadkingonthenet.com*. Yesterday, sixty-seven people posted." He goes to his backpack and pulls out a stack of paper, half an inch thick. "The Anonymous person wrote again."

He is fascinated by the Web site and Anonymous. When he shoves the papers in front of me, I read only the last few entries:

John1123: Judge O'Malley sucks! Frank Marder should be N jail 4ever! But since he's paralyzed, he gets special treatment. No fair. Meredith Stein is dead.

Maryann837: AFAICS, U can't drive drunk NTM kill someone and just WALK AWAY. You have to pay your debt to society. L

This is "walking away"?
I read to the bottom of the first page.

Anonymous: Frank Marder is a victim, too. He cannot move. Instead of punishing him, we should show him and his family mercy. Putting him in jail will not bring back Meredith Stein.

John1123: YGBK! DIKU? OT: Maryann837, R U going to practice? I need a ride.

Harry takes the printouts and puts them on the dining room table, as if I might want to look at what people are saying about me later on.

He stares.

My chin.

My neck.

The floor.

We used to talk about girls, sex, and baseball. Stats. The preseason. *Come on, Harry, speak! Let's talk like men!*

Now we sit. Harry goes back to the pictures. "You think the Sox will win the pennant?"

I don't care.

He tries again. "Or the Blue Jays? They look good."

I know Harry wishes he could take back everything that happened up until that night—he doesn't have to say it. I know he wonders if I blame him. If I ever think what might have happened if I hadn't gone to the party. If I had not talked to Meredith. If I had not . . .

Dad walks in and drunkenly drapes an arm around Harry's shoulder. Together they return to the couch. "Nice to see you, Mr. Lassiter." Dad slurs just enough to send a spit ball toward my tray. No comment. He picks up the pile of cards.

Harry is a lot more comfortable around my mom. When Dad picks up a big yellow card, a piece of poster board, folded over, Harry scoots to the edge of the couch.

Dad reads, "Harry told us in class that you're doing great. He says that you are learning to walk again. Good for you."

I can't believe it. "You told them I was learning to walk?"

"Not exactly," Harry says.

I can't help it—this makes me laugh, first a little, then a lot, then too much. I start coughing, because I don't have enough lung capacity to laugh that hard anymore. My father takes his cue to go. "I never did understand what you teenagers find so funny," and I laugh even harder, which makes me gag. Harry screams for my mother, who starts freaking out that I'm going to die right here, like a sputtering engine.

I scare them. Laughing.

They can't wig out every time I have a coughing fit. What if my leg starts spazzing out? What will Harry do then? He's supposed to be my best friend, not some zombie who eases his guilt trip by bringing pansy-ass cards from school. I don't want to see some class project full of construction paper and fear disguised as caring.

He should stop visiting me. Right now. This is not his fault. I drove the car. I hit the man. I killed Meredith. Those people are right to hate me. I'm responsible.

Only I can set him free.

"So," I begin without even a hint of a smile. "Who else do you think might want to go to Bermuda? Jocelyn?"

Harry glances at the door. "I don't know. We haven't talked about it." I smell my father's scotch.

"Really? You haven't talked about what you're doing for break? Not once?"

Sweat forms on Harry's forehead. He gathers up the cards. "No. Not yet."

Even though this is going to hurt, I do it anyway. "Listen, Harry, I really want to go. Because I need you."

"Need me?"

I don't care who hears. "Yes. I need you to hire me a hooker. Someone who will sit on my face." I take a deep breath. "You know, there are girls who will."

"My son's got a strange sense of humor," Dad says to Harry. "Real funny."

Pots clang in the kitchen. Harry looks like he wants to say something. Maybe *I'm sorry.* Maybe *Shut up.*

"I just wanted to give people hope. They feel so bad for you. They want to believe that you're going to be okay."

I wish I could stand up and beat the crap out of him. "Just get me the girl. Put me on the bed, and she'll do the rest." I sound like Freeberg on steroids. "When she's done, you can drag me into the water. Let me float. I want to die on a beautiful day in the water without this chair."

"Look, I'm sorry," Harry says. "I shouldn't have said that. But don't act like a jerk. You've still got a lot to live for. It's just hard. It's the first day."

"No! Listen to me. I've got a tube up my dick to help me pee in a bag, and nails in my neck, and no feeling anywhere south of my shoulders." Harry starts to cry. "Yeah, go ahead. Cry. Cry and walk out of here."

He goes nowhere.

"You know I can't go to Bermuda, or anywhere else. How would I get there? All I can do is sit here and wait—wait for someone like you to show up and throw some pity my way. That's my whole life. I wait, wait, wait, wait for you to visit me and pretend I'm who I used to be. The last thing I need is you telling people I'm going to get up and walk."

He blows his nose, and I almost take it all back. I almost tell him I was just playing. Except it's not a game. Not a joke. This is my life. This is the truth.

Harry doesn't give up. "Maybe you will walk. You never know. Science is making a lot of headway." He looks away and his voice trails off.

Headway. Yeah.

He strums his fingers and looks at the door. "I heard about some guy who had the same kind of injury. He learned how to use his hands. And what about your roommate?" He's losing the battle. He knows how stupid he sounds. "He can do a lot of things."

"Harry, the doctors are one hundred percent positive I'm never going to walk again." Even now, it's hard to say. What makes a man? Is it legs? Can you be a man with just a brain? "I'm never going to *do* anything again."

If I were deaf, dumb, blind, and stupid, but I could run and catch, would he be telling people at school I could learn to think again?

"Maybe you should go."

Harry gets up. He opens the door—does he know right now how lucky he is?

Yes. He knows. He knows and he wants to get out of here now. He wanted a punch line, some hope to help him, but I'm not leaving him a way out.

"I'll come back," he says. He opens the door.

No, you won't. He closes the door behind him.

Slam. Good-bye.

Game over. No winner.

"Harry's not staying for dinner?" The corners of Mom's mouth collapse. She looks like she wants to throw the plate in her hands Frisbee-style smack at my head. "Too bad," she says, answering her own question, disappearing with the plate and returning with a full glass. "I made his favorite. Lasagna."

The timer goes off. Lasagna is *my* favorite food. She downs her drink like a pro and heads back to the stove. It smells great. Hospital food sucks. I can't wait to open my mouth and let her shovel it in, one spoonful after another after another after another. My first meal at home.

I motor to the table and she turns off my power. Keep one of us at the table. How handy. She stomps over to the stairs. "Dinner!" she yells. "Now."

Dad needs one more "dinner" and two more "nows" before he manages to make an appearance at the table. He stands near his chair but does not sit.

Come on, Dad, sit and talk. Tell me a joke. "Could you move my joystick?" I ask.

He does not move. I'm not sure he knows how to do anything with my chair.

Mom puts down the salad and shows him how it's done. Her sleeve grazes the garlic bread. "Damn. Dry clean only."

Dad pulls out a magazine and stares at the center article while Mom walks back and forth, first with a salad bowl, then a white ceramic pitcher. "Water, Hal?" She fills each glass halfway. When she sits down, Dad grabs the pitcher and fills his too high; water drips on the table. Mom puts her hands together. "Thank you for the food we are about to receive." No mention of the spill.

Dad pats the table dry. "Rub-a-dub-dub. Thanks for the grub."

Pause. Silence. It's great to be home.

Mom dishes out the food, first to Dad, then to me. Her plate remains empty. She grabs my fork from my place setting, and scoops up some lasagna. She places it in my mouth, holding a napkin under my chin, just in case she pulls the fork out too fast. No one tells her to fill her plate; no one reminds her to eat.

"It's so fine to have you home, Frank," my father says.

I let the food settle on my tongue, then chew: cheese and sauce, but no meat. A minor disappointment. "Thanks, Dad."

Mom delivers another mouthful into the back of my throat. This time, she gives me meat, pasta, and sauce, and an oversized chunk of onion, but no cheese. No cheese. She says, "Father Joseph called today. He's going to try to stop by, but he's so busy. I was thinking we should call the taxi and see him at church. What do you think?"

Dad stuffs his face with lasagna. "How much does it cost?"

Mom sighs. It must cost a lot, because she drops the subject. "He said there were three new admits." She holds the cup in my face and sticks the straw in my mouth. "Such a shame. Such a shame. One was a girl. Fell off her bike in traffic. No helmet." Mom takes every injury personally.

Dad shovels food into his mouth. "How stupid can you be?"

"One of the boys was injured in a forty-two-car pileup on the interstate. Did you hear about that?" She stuffs a bite in my mouth. Cheese and meat. Zucchini. I hate when she adds vegetables.

Spoonful after spoonful. Cheese and meat. Cheese and pasta. Statistically, she's got to get it right some time. Meat and cheese. Sauce, pasta, and onion. But no. No. She does not get it right. She messes it up. Every time.

"Four people died. In the pileup." Sauce and pasta. More zucchini. Nothing to drink. Where's the bread? The salad?

"Do it right!" I yell. "Can't you do it right? A little bit of everything. Pasta, cheese, sauce, and meat. How stupid are you? Why can't you do it the way I like it?"

Mom begins to cry.

"Nice, Frank," Dad says. He downs his second or third scotch. "You could try being a little polite." He pushes back from the table, gets up, and disappears. My mother throws my napkin on the ground and leaves the table, too. The half-finished dinner sits on the table.

"Do you think this is fun for me?" I am stuck; the chair won't move. "I can't even pick up a fork and eat my food."

Come back.

Please, come back. Don't leave.

Someone.

Television noise blares from above. The door slams. The smell of garlic teases me, makes me tired. I close my eyes and wait.

Her ice-cold hand stings my neck. "Sorry, Frank," Mom says. She turns on the power and puts my joystick back in place, enabling the chair.

I smell the stale remains of Italian dressing and sauce. I must have fallen asleep, zoned out—not sure how long. The sun looks almost red; it stabs the clouds and makes them bleed.

"Do you want me to reheat your dinner?"

"No, no thanks."

She stacks the plates and heads for the kitchen. She does not invite me to join her, she does not encourage me to talk.

She needs a break.

Me, too. Have chin, will travel.

My bedroom is now off the living room in the room we used to call the den, a straight drive from the dinner table. All my old furniture is present and accounted for, but it is newly clean and my papers are gone. No clutter; my CDs are in order. There is no dust, no book set aside carelessly for later. Just like the wall in the living room, this place feels like old country music, wailing and crying for something that is gone. The life has been sucked out of it. My father should make a brass plate: Frank Marder's bedroom, circa 2007.

I motor to face the desk and smell pine, Lysol pine. And Murphy oil soap. My mother dusts twice a week. Tuesdays and Fridays, every week, all year.

The bed, a brand-spanking-new hospital-issue bed, takes up most of the space. They bought a special skin-saving mattress so they won't have to roll me every two hours. The special pillow is in place, too. The white-and-yellow blanket looks soft. I wonder if it matters. It could be the roughest, most uncomfortable, scratchiest blanket on the planet, and what would I care?

My old blanket was blue-green. I picked it out last year—big sale at the outlet. Mom made me go. She told me to buy a good one. For college.

Harry rode shotgun. We put our hands on every blanket in the store and imagined all the girls that we'd get to know underneath them. College was going to make us men. College was going to bring us girls. College was the place where there were more of them than us.

After a few more fantasies, I paid for a blanket with a thick satin border that felt great under my chin. Ironic. I got the matching sheets, too. I always loved sleeping late and lying under the covers. Meredith did, too.

Once.

"You look good in green," I said.

She was up to her chin in my blankets and me.

"This feels so good," she said, squirming around until there was no air between her skin and mine. "I feel like I'm swimming in silk."

I kissed the back of her head, pleased with myself, confident that I'd soon be getting the payoff I'd imagined.

Sleeping late. Not on my schedule.

Swimming in silk. Never again.

Girl in my bed.

Once.

Mom comes in. "Is it okay?"

"Yes. It's very nice." Her eyes are expectant, needy. She has worked hard to make the space right.

"You have a speakerphone here," she says, waving her arm in the direction of the desk, "and we just ordered a special intercom and a new computer. Voice-activated." She waits for me to say something affirmative.

"Yes. Good." Damn. My voice lacks enthusiasm. The day has already been too hard. A voice-activated computer is a great thing. A speakerphone, too. Great consolation prizes. *Sorry you can't move, Frank. Sorry you picked the wrong door. But here are the gimp toys, just for you. Ladies and gentlemen, let's give Frank a hand!*

Tomorrow. I will tell her thank you tomorrow, when I can really mean it, when I can push out more than one syllable at a time.

She wants it now. *Now, Frank, now.*

"I tried to put every poster in its place."

Yes, yes, yes, the posters are all here, the ripped corners repaired with invisible tape. You can still see where she took off the tape, the tape I was not supposed to put on the newly painted walls so many years and months and weeks ago. I know. I see. I'll tell her tomorrow.

Now. Now.

"I went through every book. I brought down your trophies and your old model planes."

"Thanks."

"We bought the new bed. We fixed the bathroom. We did everything they told us."

"Mom."

"Frank." She sits on my bed.

"What did you do with my room upstairs?" Shit, my head wants to explode. I don't know why I'm asking this. She should call my dad and get me in bed.

"I turned it into an all-purpose room," she says. "Like an office, with a small TV and a treadmill." Pause. Frown.

"A family room?"

"Not really." Her lips pucker. She is biting the inside of her mouth.

A family room by any other name is still a family room. For the walking people in the house. A sanctuary, away from me. I bet it looks great, full of color and comfy chairs and shelves full of books that you can pick up with your hands and read. She can pucker her lips all she wants; she is going to stand there and tell me all about it.

"What color did you paint it?"

"Celery stalk." My mother glances back at the door. "With a splash of glaze and celadon."

"What kind of treadmill? The one with arms? What about the furniture? The TV? Is it a flat screen? How many inches?" I am an asshole. My mother is going to need a place to go. I shouldn't take it out on her, but I do. I do. I wanted those things, too. I still want them.

"I brought everything down." She takes two steps away from me. "Every book, every card, every poster, Frank. I tried to make this space nice. I did the best I could." She looks over her shoulder again, but Dad is not going to come to her rescue.

My favorite books, the ones I will never pick up and read again, are here. Alphabetized. The stereo, the model airplane from seventh grade, the trophy for winning last year's science fair are all in place. Just the dust is gone.

"Where is it?" I ask. Her cheeks turn red. She knows what I want.

"Your card collection is in the top drawer. Do you want to see it?" She is ready to mobilize. She will show me each card if she has to.

"No. No cards, Mom. I want the jar."

"Let me get Dad. You need to get to bed."

She looks away. "Did you throw it away?" *Pride* and *privacy* are just words. I am not ashamed.

The look on her face makes me wish I hadn't asked. Call it disappointment. Call it fear. She crosses herself and clears her throat.

"Are you talking about the old pickle jar containing four used condoms?"

Meredith dubbed it "the candy jar." We were going to see how fast we could fill it.

"Yes. That jar."

Mom looks over her shoulder again, but Dad, her husband, the person she probably wanted to initiate this talk, is not here. "No. It is not here. I threw it away. When I found it, I—" She sniffs. "I thought I raised you better than that. I thought you were a respectful young man. I thought you were different . . ." She starts crying. "What you did—what you saved—it was repulsive. I didn't even know you were . . . I thought you were different . . . than your father."

I don't have the energy to be mad. I was not like my father. I was just having fun. The jar is gone. Screaming won't bring it back. For that matter, seeing the jar won't bring me back.

"It was mine." My voice sounds weak.

"It was revolting," she says.

Once I was a boy who became a man. Then I was a man who became a head. The jar was just a jar.

They should have let me die. They should have put the period at the end of the sentence that is me, my life, my time. They had at least ten good reasons. They probably had that many opportunities.

But nobody did it. Nobody ever started counting.

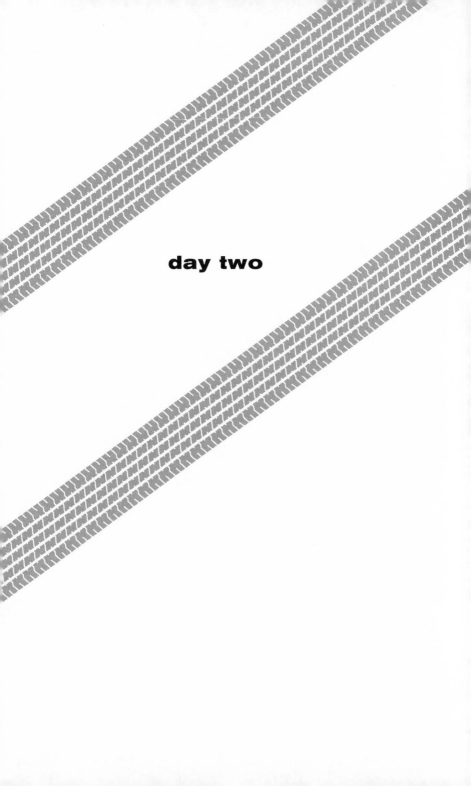

day two

You can tell right away that Sunset Goldberg wasn't always an employee of the state. Her hair is braided in long, skinny purple, pink, and yellow braids that hang to the middle of her back. She wears a big green rock in her nose and a red string around her wrist.

My mother brings her decaf chai tea. "Next time, I'll make sure to have soymilk."

"Frank, my job is to oversee your transition from hospital to home," Sunset says.

Mom nods. *Yes, yes, thank you, thank you for helping me with this unbearable burden.*

"You can ask me anything. I'm a licensed occupational therapist, as well as your care coordinator. Periodically, I will report your needs to the state." Sunset blows on her tea before she sips. "But that's mostly a formality. Be confident that we'll get you all the equipment that you need as fast as we possibly can."

"Have you heard anything about the van?" Mom's watch beeps, and she gets off the couch. Time to shift my weight.

Sunset motions my mother to stand to the side. Together, they tip my head forward until I can see my knees. "I'll grab Frank's back, you keep him steady. I'd like to take a quick look at his skin. Just to make sure." She takes a deep breath. "On *three*." They pull me up, just out of the chair.

"I feel a little light-headed."

"We got you," Sunset says. Mom hums.

"Looking good, *look-ing* good." My pants rustle when she pulls them back up; my body thumps when it hits the chair. "Frank, think of me as your navigator. I'll find help for your mother, a therapist who will come to the house, and will be available twenty-four–seven to answer your questions." She puts me down and brings her mug to her lips.

"You want some water?" Mom asks. Sweat rolls down Sunset's blouse.

"Thanks, yes. Don't worry about the van. It will be ready soon."

She'd sound very professional if it wasn't for the hair and the string and the funny accent. "Are you from France?" Great language, French.

"No," Sunset says. "I grew up in the Bronx. I lived in Toulouse for three years. My boyfriend grew up there. I guess I have one of those voices that picks up new accents." She finishes her tea. Puts up a finger. *"Je vais retourner tout suite!"*

"Back in a flash," I translate.

Mom stands at the window and we watch Sunset unload boxes from her car. "Careful," my mother says, "you don't want to drop that."

My computer.

"Careful, you don't want to drop that."

The fancy new intercom.

"Careful—"

Sunset smiles at me. "I won the Miss New York power-lifting championship three years ago. Came in tenth in the nationals. I can deadlift three hundred and thirty-five pounds clean. Don't you worry. I won't drop anything."

She may be able lift a computer, but she does not have the intuition to install the software. She hunts and pecks and curses for two hours. Mom sits in the living room and reads. I motor back and forth between them. Can't the state find someone who can read a goddamn manual?

"Isn't it time to shift my weight?" Mom gets up from the table like I'm an impatient toddler who wants the same answer to a question that has been answered before.

How many more minutes, Mom? Huh, Mom?

Sunset fumbles for another half hour before suggesting we break for lunch. She watches my mother feed me, just to make sure that our transition to home hasn't caused her to forget how to shovel tiny bits of food into my mouth. She feeds me leftover lasagna; every bite is perfectly balanced.

When I am full, Mom brings out a fancy salad for two. And sparkling lemonade with slivers of lime floating on the top. Flat bread. Strawberries and cream.

"This salad is so delicious, Mrs. Marder. Jean Pierre makes one like it, except he likes mandarin oranges instead of raisins."

"How lovely that your boyfriend cooks."

What's wrong with raisins?

"Jean Pierre makes the best crepes. I know it sounds like a stereotype—French guy, crepes—but it's true. I'll bring some next time."

Mom plays with her hair as she eats. She shovels the food into her mouth too fast, and she comments "Ah yes" and "To be sure" in her high-pitched voice. From the sound of things, Jean Pierre would be perfect if only he had a job, but hell, for a good crepe, Sunset's willing to forgive him. He even does the dishes. I bet he's a great lover.

My father does not prepare any food. He does no dishes. He's a good lover, too, I'm sure, but I bet my mother is thinking that now she wishes he wasn't so good. She shovels even faster.

"We do what we have to do," she says.

Sunset nods and smiles. "Yes, we do, we sure do." She doesn't understand that my mother is warning her. My mother gets no pleasure doing what she has to do.

Shovel, shovel, shovel.

They finish lunch and slog through the final steps to download the software.

"This is your key to accessibility," Sunset says. She seems very proud of herself.

She's wrong. It is entertainment, something to keep me busy.

"I thought my chair was the key to my—"

"Frank." My mother puts her hand over her mouth.

Sunset says, "You'll be able to receive and send your schoolwork from here. You'll be able to write. All you have to do is speak. It will do anything you say."

Fine, fine, fine.

Sunset rubs her hands together. "Frank, why don't you try it out? Say something. Say a couple of things. Just speak into the microphone and it will do the work."

"Normal voice?" I'm stalling. The last thing I need is an audience.

"Come on, Frank. Try it. You're going to love it. This machine will do anything you say."

"Later."

"Now."

An ambulance drives by. No one says anything until the siren fades.

"Okay," I say. Sunset smiles. Mom leans over my chair. Her hair tickles my ear. "Walk."

Mom frowns. "He's always like that now," she says, like I'm not sitting here, in the room, with the two of them. "Cheeky."

Sunset sympathizes. "His attitude is normal and understandable. A trauma like this affects the whole family. Frank needs time to heal. So do you. Be patient. There will be hard days ahead. But remember, each day you will discover something new. Each day, Frank will overcome a new hurdle, just the way he did when he was able-bodied."

"Easy for you to say." I hate when people talk about me like I'm not sitting there listening.

My mother throws up her hands. "He used to be a quiet, polite kid. I raised him to be respectful."

Sunset does not look surprised or insulted. "Give him time," she says. "Every story has a beginning. This is his."

Wrong again.

My story begins with a phone call. Harry, who else? He knew I was home, licking my wounds. Betsy Sinclair and I were through—she broke up with me, two weeks earlier, in front of a small audience at the Mooretown Marauders soccer game. It could have been much more humiliating, but honestly, her desertion did not mean much. She was a skinny, vain girl who thought, for a moment in time, that I would elevate her social status.

Silly girl. I was a regular guy. Not popular, not a jerk. In the middle. Elevation potential: zero.

"Come on. It's the party at the park. A perfect occasion to get back in the saddle." He was serious.

"No," I said. "I don't want to see her."

"Frank," he went on, "everyone will be there." It was true. The junior/senior picnic was the kickoff party of the year.

I sighed. "So go. Have fun." Harry was quiet on the other end. "Harry, I really don't feel like it. You know how much I hate sitting in the sun."

"Let me remind you," he said. "I suffered through six weeks of Accutane. Six weeks." He stopped talking, probably checking e-mail at the same time. "For parties. And invitations to them. Come on, Marder. Jocelyn Manis called me. She asked if we were going."

"No one's stopping you."

"Frank, Jocelyn Manis. Asked. Me. Don't let me down. I want to get laid *before* we graduate."

I was acting like a jerk, making him beg.

"Come on, man. You know you want to go. You just need me to give you a reason."

"No, I don't."

"Frank, I can't go alone. I don't have anything to say."

Deep breath.

"I'd go for you."

I let him wait a little longer. The sun was shining. The breeze was light. Harry was my best friend.

"I think we've had enough for a while," Sunset says. "Why don't I help you into bed for an hour?"

"No thanks. I'd like to stay up and work on the computer. Maybe have another can of Coke." Mom does not get up to get it.

"Frank, I'm really glad you're so enthusiastic, but actually, you need to go down," Sunset says. "Just for a bit. You've been in the chair for a long time. Give your butt a break. You don't want to get a bedsore." She pushes my chair to the bed and locks it tight. Power-play takedown for Sunset! Bedsore lecture will follow if compliance is not forthcoming. "I imagine that the hardest thing you have to deal with is giving up some control."

Oh yeah, control is right up there on the crip's big list of favorite things that he doesn't have anymore.

"But once we get your schedule down, you'll find that you'll get at least some of it back. You'll know your body. You'll know your limits. You can tell us . . ."

Now, later, whenever. Blah, blah, blah. She can do whatever she wants to me. She can pick me up and throw me across the room, or she can leave me here. That's never going to change. Even the stupid things like going to bed—Sunset doesn't understand.

"I know my body now. I don't want to go to bed."

Sunset smiles and shakes her head. "Sorry, bud, but your mom and I are putting you down." She grabs me by the hips. Mom stands by, but doesn't really do anything except look nervous. "Get on the bed," Sunset says, "and when I sit him down, you support his back with your body." She takes a deep breath. "This is gonna be fun."

One, two . . .

"Sunset, I want to stay in my chair."

Three . . .

"Sunset, I mean it."

Up.

They've got me sitting on this stupid bed. Sitting. In space. I can't see Mom's hands around my chest, but I can feel her breath, short and fast on the back of my neck. "Put me down," I say. "Now. Back in the chair. This isn't funny. You can't just push me around like a doll."

"It's good for you," Sunset says. Her hands are shaking; her muscles are popping out of her skinny arms. Power lifter, my ass. She's going to drop me.

"Mom?"

"Right here." She sounds scared. "I've got you." Her hair grazes my neck. Why can't she be in front? Why are they doing this?

"You look great, Frank," Sunset says, and then without warning, Mom gasps, and my body collapses, and my head hits the pillow as Sunset pushes me down on my side.

"Oh no!" Mom holds on to me so I don't slip off the edge. "I'm sorry. So, so sorry." She kisses my face. "I couldn't hold on."

The floor looks very far away.

People who are shot, people who are about to die in airplanes—scientists say that their neurological systems turn off. They go into shock. They feel no pain. If I hit the floor, will mine turn on?

Will I feel a moment of searing pain through my body? Will a bolt of sensation go through me, just before my head hits the floor?

It would be worth it.

Sunset tries to get me up, but my leg starts spazzing out, so they just hold me there, on the edge of the bed, on my side. More helpless than usual. Scared.

"Don't worry, Rosemary. Frank's fine."

No, no, no—I'm not fine. From now on, I'm deciding when and how to go to bed.

A blue piece of paper is stuck under the leg of my nightstand.

When my leg stops shaking, Sunset sits me back up. "You okay, Frank?" She doesn't wait for an answer. She grabs me and lays me out on the bed. "No harm done. Before I go, we'll get him back up in the chair."

Mom covers me with a blanket. She sits on the edge of the bed and hums until she thinks I'm asleep. On the ceiling is one of Dad's old posters from college—some chick with big hair in a bathing suit. He said, "Every fantasy I had at your age was about her. Wasn't she a knockout?"

He must have put it up there to entertain me, but it just takes me back to August and the park.

The party was in full swing. Skin everywhere. People talking and laughing. Faces. Legs. Chests. Footballs flying through the air. I froze on the sidelines, still as a statue, unable or unwilling. My classmates were all having fun. It was a sunny, breezy day. We were seniors. They made it look so easy.

"How's it going?"

"What'd you do all summer?"

"Where are you applying?"

Harry took a swig of root beer. "There she is," he said, looking into the crowd. "Do I look okay? Am I breaking out?"

"What are you, a girl?" I shook my head. "Go on ahead. I'll find you later."

He didn't hesitate. Long hair, floppy hats, shaved heads, and other assorted lids swallowed his blue baseball cap. I scanned the crowd for familiar faces and watched him greet Jocelyn, expecting her to smile, blow him off. I figured he'd be sitting next to me momentarily. But instead, she put her hands on his shoulders.

Jocelyn Manis was bursting out of a very skimpy bikini. Damn. The guy was going to beat me to the Promised Land.

I grabbed a hot dog off the grill and sat down on a swing. Put my towel on my lap. There was plenty of time to socialize.

"Nice party, huh?" she asked.

Meredith Stein had her brown hair pulled up in a tangle of a ponytail, and her aviator sunglasses were mirrored. She was hotter than Betsy—ten times hotter—and completely out of my league. I looked past her smile to see if maybe my ex-girlfriend was looking this way.

"Yeah," I said, wiping my lip for potential mustard residue. Checking my fingers. Thinking about my shorts, my chest. I was too white, too concave, too obviously unaccustomed to socializing. "How's it going? What'd you do all summer? Where are you applying?"

Meredith laughed. "You sound like a reporter." She extended her hand, and I put mine in hers, and she took me into the crowd to finish our conversation.

Meredith Stein was holding my hand. My hand, holding my hand, she was holding my hand and we were talking, or rather, she was talking.

"My summer was great. At my camp, the summer before senior year, you get to be a CIT—I mean, counselor-in-training. I worked with eleven-year-old girls. I couldn't believe it—all they wanted to do was wash and blow-dry their hair."

We were nearly shoulder to shoulder, eye to eye, hip to hip, and she was holding my hand.

"Really."

"I know! This one kid had scoliosis, and so she had to wear a brace, and it was so sad. For Fourth of July, I let her take it off, so she could hang with her boyfriend. Isn't that cute?"

"Yeah." She could talk all day, as long as she kept holding my hand.

She had freckles on every inch of her skin. Her face, her shoulders, her chest, her legs. She had muscular legs. Great legs. I tried to keep my eyes moving, head nodding, so she couldn't tell how obviously excited I was to be standing there, looking at her, listening to her talk. Eyes, breasts, hair, breasts, tummy . . . she had a belly ring. Gold. A cloud obscured the sun, and she shivered. "Brrrr. When the sun goes in, it gets so cold."

"Yeah," I said. "Yeah." Let the sun go in. Let it get real cold. Her nipples were visible through her top.

She stood there, making words, talking to me, like we knew

each other, like we were friends. "What's your favorite class?" She had great lips, too. Full, hot pink lips. Shiny. The bridge of her nose was starting to peel. Her shoulders looked burned, too. I wished I could concentrate on what she was saying. "Someone told me you like to play baseball."

"Yes, I like baseball." I didn't understand why she was so interested in me. My internal alarm was clanging, screaming, telling me to run, get out of there, go to the bathroom, away. "But I don't play for the team. Just for fun. What do you like to do?"

What is the thing that doesn't go with the others? There was something happening here. She asked more questions: "Who's your favorite band? Do you like art? Have you been to the MFA in Boston?"

"I like Sargent," I said, but she didn't hear me through the blast of a bullhorn. She pointed to her ear, shrugged her shoulders, and mouthed, "Later." Then she tapped another guy on the shoulder.

"Nice meeting you," I said. "Maybe I'll call you sometime."

"Huh? What did you say? You got a partner yet?" John Guttman introduced himself and started firing questions like bullets.

It was a mixer, a game meant for people like them to draw in people like me. After Guttman, I went back to the swings and watched. The bullhorn blasted again and again.

"Isn't this great?" Harry asked. His cheeks were bright pink.

"You forgot to put on sunscreen."

Harry laughed. "Jocelyn Manis talked to me for three separate rotations. Three times. She says I crack her up. She says—"

Meredith Stein appeared out of the crowd. A T-shirt wrapped around her head turban-style. Bikini top. That gold ring like a bull's eye on her bare belly. A big pink towel wrapped around her hips. I stared at her yellow flip-flops. "Are you coming?" She put her finger under my chin and lifted my face.

"Absolutely," Harry said without consultation. "See you at camp in twenty minutes."

"Camp?" I asked. "Where is camp?"

Meredith laughed. "My family owns this big piece of property. We call it *camp*. Weren't you listening? I invited you to a postparty party."

It took us forty-five minutes to find the right field. "You made it," she said. "I wasn't sure." She kissed both of us on the lips. Meredith Stein tasted like cheap beer and potato chips. "Come over to the bonfire," she said.

Harry licked his lips. "Jocelyn's here." He patted me on the back. Second time in three hours. "Have fun."

Meredith handed me a beer. "Loosen up," she said, tipping back her own can. "Have fun."

I took the beer.

She walked away.

I didn't drink it. Not that day.

As promised, Sunset puts me back in my chair just in time for the Parade of State-Supported Ladies. They all start the same way: "Hi, Frank, can I talk to your mom a minute?" Then they go *hush-hush* into the living room to talk strategy. As if they are talking about things I have never heard before.

Mobility, skin, my mother's health.

Skin, my mother's health, mobility.

My mother's health, mobility, skin.

Victoria, the physical therapist, is the third person on the schedule. She barges into the living room fast, then stops *bam*, and wipes her brow. "I thought I was going to be late," she says. Victoria is one of those super-cutesy girls—pink-and-orange T-shirt and cute raggy jeans, torn at both knees. Short, short hair. Her purse is covered with buttons: PEACE, LOVE, AND UNDERSTAND-ING. MY BOYFRIEND IS A DEMOCRAT. SAVE THE WHALES.

"Okay, Frank Marder. Let's talk," she says, sitting in front of me, legs wide open, elbows on her thighs. "I want to know what you have done, and if you've experienced any changes. I want to know everything. A twitch. A pain. I'm an unadulterated optimist, and I don't mind saying so. You know, people like you sometimes get as much as a level back. Why I once worked with a patient . . ."

She talks continuously. ". . . I can't tell you his name—confidentiality and all—but this one guy spent seventeen days in a coma only to wake up and start walking. Then I also had this other guy who wouldn't stop masturbating." She rolls her eyes as if masturbating was the most unheard-of activity on the planet. "Every time I walked into his room, there he was . . ." She makes the standard gesture. "He was always going at it." She laughs. My mother laughs. But it's not funny. I'd give more than a big chunk of change for one more hour in my bedroom with a functioning wrist and a hard-on.

"I think what Victoria is saying, is that if you are determined, you might be able to learn something."

Victoria nods vigorously, making her gigantic breasts wobble. "Feel free to ask me anything," she says. "Anything. Especially sex stuff." She does not turn red, but my mother does. "I wrote my master's thesis on sexuality and the paralyzed male. There are still a lot of things you can do with a lover. Believe me, you can still have sex. And not just oral sex, although that alone is pretty satisfying for any partner."

My mother is still in the room.

"You do have a functioning tongue, I presume."

My mother leaves the room. "I can see I'm not needed," she says on her way out.

Victoria won't drop the subject. "I work with this one guy who's got the same injury you have. And he has a very active sex life."

I laugh, but she's not joking. She reaches over and behind me and shifts my weight.

"Save your talk for your other guy. I can't feel anything. It doesn't work."

"Have you tried?"

"How am I supposed to try? Ask my mom? Or a nurse?"

She's making me mad. "You want to rub my dick so we can see what's up?"

Victoria doesn't insult easily. "I wasn't suggesting that. But have you tried thinking sexy thoughts? Imagining someone beautiful?"

"Nothing happens."

"Are you sure?" she asks.

She's pissing me off. "Look," I say in as controlled a voice as possible, "I am done with sex. I can't do anything. I can't feel anything. No one is going to drop out of the sky to fuck me." I wish my mom would come back and tell her to leave.

Victoria says, "I'm going to stretch your ankles in the chair. Then we'll get you into bed to stretch your legs and arms." She drops out of sight. I think she's done lecturing, but no. No. I'm trapped in the chair—Sex for Crips 101. "Frank, a lot of guys with quadriplegia start out thinking they have to punish themselves. But they're wrong. You *can* have a sex life. There are things we can discuss with your doctor—erectile drugs—one may work. My other guy gets his girl to inject vasoactive drugs into his—"

"Inject?"

"Yeah. Inject. Or if you're squirrelly about needles, your partner can try using a vibrator. Or you can go for the vacuum-induced erection. The pump literally inflates your—"

"Okay. I get it." Freeberg would love this girl. "But you keep forgetting one thing. I can't feel anything."

"Frank, sexuality is not just about feeling your dick. Yes, you can't feel it. That's a drag. You're probably not going to be able to have much of an orgasm either. And you're going to have issues keeping it up. But love and affection can be expressed in lots of ways. You might find that your earlobes become very sensitive. Or your scalp." She waits for me to demonstrate shock or enthusiasm.

But all I am is mad and frustrated. "Who's going to date me?" Really. Who? Between the chair and the smell and the obvious mobility issues, I'm gross. "I need help doing everything. No one is going to want to talk to me, let alone get naked and put a vacuum around my dick and pump."

"You don't think so now. But once you're used to things, we can go out on the town. Meet people. Next time you're on your computer, I'll show you some SCI chat sites. You'll learn a lot." She stands up so I can see her wink.

She doesn't get it.

"I'm not going to be your little science project. In case you've forgotten, this is my life. And it's a non-issue. I don't want to talk about it. No one is going to go out with me. I killed two people."

She follows me to my room, and transfers me onto the bed. I smell like bad meat.

"You know, I read a lot about you in the paper. A few times, I posted on one of those sites."

"Don't tell me. You're Anonymous."

"No, but I agree with her or him. The paper was pretty harsh, the way they treated you. I mean, they can't exactly take care of you in jail, can they? I mean, even though you are guilty."

"Can we change the topic?"

"Really, who's going to shift your weight? And they're not exactly going to give you the right bed. Seriously. They can't provide enough."

"Can we—"

"And your poor girlfriend . . . Do you miss her? Do you think about her? Did you love her?"

"No, I didn't love her." Victoria's face drops. Wrong answer, clearly, because she says nothing else. "We had just started dating."

Victoria nods, but when she begins to stretch my deadwood, she still looks disappointed. I want to shout, "Why is it so important that I loved her? Does it make my story better? Will someone go out with me? Will I get the erection, the great new life, or at least the mercy fuck? If I loved her, do you like me more?"

If I loved her, will everyone leave me alone?

I didn't love her. But I did like her a lot, a whole lot. Her liking me felt like a reward for being the nice, smart, rule-abiding person that I had always been. Finally—the nice kid won. Justice. She was like an unbelievably pleasant dream.

She should have been a fun chapter in my book of life. We could have kept in touch, hooked up on school breaks. You hear about people like that.

If I hadn't gone to the party, maybe we'd still be okay.

Victoria finishes stretching my legs. She puts me back in my chair in time for the nurse to deal with my excrement and body fluids.

I wish I had loved Meredith.

Mom is on the phone with the hospital. She has detected the beginnings of a bedsore on my upper right thigh, outer not inner, doctor, and she wants someone to look at me. No, she can't wait until Sunset comes tomorrow. Yes, she stretched me. Yes, she did not keep me in the chair all day. Yes, she is worried. No, it is more than pink. It is red. "Red!" she yells. "Red! His ass is red, goddamnit!" Send a doctor, her baby is dying. She should only be so lucky.

My inbox is empty. The George Washington science club's site is outdated. They haven't posted anything new for two weeks. *Quadking*, however, is current. Harry was right, it gets a lot of hits.

> *Check out this link to an interview with one of Frank Marder's occupational therapists. Learn what he regrets, what he misses most, what he says about Meredith Stein.*

This is such bullshit. I never talked about Meredith to anyone.

Mark92: WTF???? Y is FM still free? FYI, my mom's cousin is a judge in Az. He said that NFW would he let someone like FM pass go.

Joann888: PMFJI, but who cares what he misses most! He's a jerk and a killer, and it MAKES ME SICK that he is living at home, in his nice house, in his nice neighborhood, and she is DEAD!

Anonymous: Do you really think Frank Marder has gotten off free? He is paralyzed from the neck down. If that isn't jail, I don't know what is. Why are people so concerned about him? His life is ruined. Leave him alone.

Anonymous may be the last person in cyberspace who understands me. From the next room, my mother continues to freak out about my skin. "I don't know how long he's been in the chair. Yes. He spent an hour in the bed. Is that enough? What are you saying?"

The front door slams shut. Dad is home. He comes straight here. Smart man. "Hey, Frank, how's it going?" He loosens his tie. "Tell your mom—"

"Tell me what?" She's got the best radar on the planet. The phone is probably still hot in her hand. Dad takes the full drink from the other. The ice tinkles.

"Big meeting tonight, Rosemary." Never a good sign.

She barricades the door. "Hal, you've got to take a look at him. Now."

My mother is still clutching the phone in her hand. He downs his drink in one gulp and slams the empty glass onto the dresser. More tinkling.

"Okay, let's take a look." The phone rings. Before Mom can answer, he grabs that, too. He stuffs it under his arm and reaches over my head to heave me forward out of the chair, just the way Cecilia used to. He's got his knees bracing my legs, his shoes are untied. *Ring, ring.* He holds me there, looking, smelling. My ass, my back. *Ring, ring.* He snorts. Stagnant skin stinks. He smells like cologne and alcohol. He's never done a skin check before. When the ringing stops, he puts me back in the chair.

It always takes a moment for my head to feel right.

"What do you think?" My mother taps her foot while he makes a call.

"Yes . . . yes . . . this is Hal Marder. Uh-huh. He's fine," he says. "A little pink. I think I'll put him back in the bed early. Is that okay?" He sounds credible. He does not stutter. No *ums* or pauses. He speaks in simple terms, and unlike my mother, he listens. "I'll ask Sunset to take a look at the chair tomorrow. She can make sure everything's in place." He puts the phone down hard on the table. Next to the glass.

Two days home and already she is calling the hospital, worrying about the chair, checking for skin problems. He untucks his shirt, takes off his tie and drapes it over the dresser. Two days home and he is out of here. "You look fine, Frank. Rosemary, you can't panic like this." He starts unbuttoning his shirt. "I gotta go. Can't be late."

"What if you're wrong?" she asks, scooping up the tie, rolling it between her fingers until it is a tight ball in her hand. "What if he gets a sore?"

"Then he'll go back to the hospital." My father's voice sounds tense; he does not like missing dinner meetings.

"Look again," she says. "Maybe I didn't shift him enough. Maybe we should bring him in. You know what they said." She throws the tie on the floor.

Yeah. They said it would be good for me to go home. That it

would boost my morale. They said I would be more comfortable at home.

Bullshit. Sitting in my house all day, waiting for the therapists, looking at my television instead of the hospital set, is not better. They should have said it would be good for them. Because it's not good for me to be stuck here with my neurotic mother and distracted father.

Dad picks up the tie and stuffs it into my top drawer. "I'll be back late," he says, sliding past my chair, waving, walking out, not touching. My mother follows him. Since I can't see my thigh, inner or outer, at this very moment, I refuse to get sucked up in this hysteria. *Quadking* stares at me. Since my dad got home, two more people have posted. One thinks I'm faking.

Mom calls, "Frank, let me know when you want some dinner."

The other post has to do with God and original sin and whether or not I am the devil himself. I recheck my inbox. Still empty. "Shut down." The computer responds. Maybe there's something good on TV. Maybe I'll e-mail Harry tomorrow.

Mom has the remote; she is struggling to set up her new DVR. Today Sunset showed her how to record her soaps, but already, she is confused. When the show is finally rolling, she notices me. "Want to eat in here?" Halsted, the lifelong matriarch of the show, just found out her long-lost daughter is none other than Tiffany Reese, the slut who just bedded Halsted's son.

Escape reality.

Dad heads for the door. "Don't wait up," he says. Slam.

Mom brings dinner to me. "It will be fun to eat while we watch TV."

Escape. "Can you believe that Tiffany Reese is Halsted's daughter? This show is so unbelievable."

Tonight, I don't complain about the food.

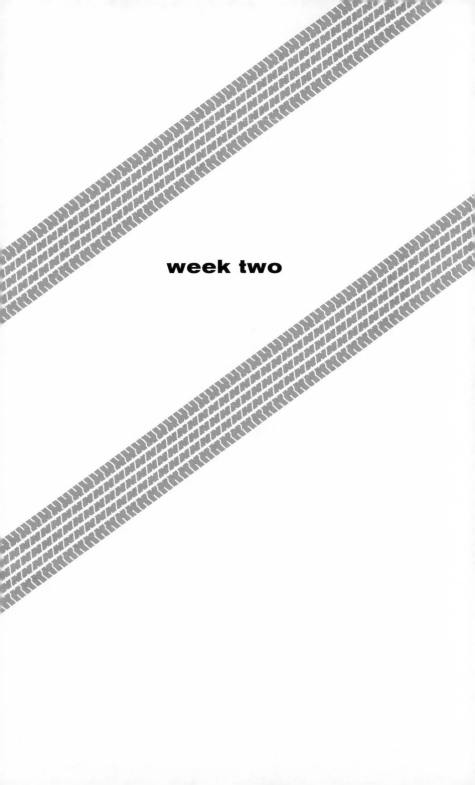

week two

You would think that sleeping would be the one thing a crip like me could still do, but believe it or not, it's not easy. My room is too dark, too quiet. The shades block out everything, even the streetlights. In the hospital, the room was bright and noisy. Even at night, there were lights and sounds, people walking down the halls, talking and laughing. I knew where I was all the time.

Here, my bed could be a coffin. Underground. It is late. No one is awake but me.

The blackness covers me, squeezes me. Panic. I feel nauseous; I need some light. Lying here in the nothingness, I can't make out anything, not the ceiling or the side of the bed or the landmarks that prove this is my room. Mom should have left the hall light on. She should ask me before leaving me like this. There should be a sliver of light—one sliver. One goddamn sliver.

Someone should at least come in and check on me.

One, two, three. I count to ten, then fifteen. Maybe if I count to one hundred, my eyes will get used to not seeing, the way my body is used to not feeling. Twenty, twenty-one. My head will not stop spinning. Thirty-five, thirty-six; my mom needs to sleep. The intercom is on. If I yell, she'll come down. She'll turn on the lights.

Even the appliances don't tick.

Victoria comes at nine in the morning, occupational therapy's at ten. Sleep is imperative. The blanket under my chin is soft.

Meredith kisses me on the forehead. "You are too uptight," she whispers. "Relax. Enjoy the darkness. Hold my hand."

Early September, we went to the movies. Her head was on my shoulder, her hair tickled my neck, her shoulder touched mine. My thigh did not move. I could not risk my thigh touching hers. We were not yet a couple. I liked her, but I thought she was just being friendly. Harry disagreed. He said Meredith told him I was cute.

"Not hot?" We laughed.

"No. Cute. And funny."

Did not.

Did too.

Did not.

Girls like her do not like boys like me. Girls like her like guys with muscles, hairy chests, and strong arms. Boys like me do not talk to girls like her.

Girls who like boys like me are smart. They're in the drama club, they're the substitutes on the debate team. Girls who like boys like me do not carry condoms. They walk down the halls without being recognized. They do not look anything like Meredith Stein.

Do too.

When the movie ended, she didn't leave her seat. She stared at the screen. "Every one of those people helped make that movie," she said, "but nobody cares. Nobody even bothers reading their names."

"Absolutely. Nobody cares." I tried to sound indignant. There was no way I wanted to get up yet.

After the last credit, the room became quiet and dark. She grabbed my hand and kissed me on the lips. My tongue found hers, or maybe hers found mine. Her hand reached around my neck and massaged my head, twirled my mess of curls. She said, "Frank Marder, you have beautiful hair." I felt a knot in my stomach.

"Meredith." She is gone.

In my room, in the darkness, I try to feel that moment, that knot, the thrill. Maybe the blackness of the room can offer me memory.

My mother turns on the light and walks in, frantic. "Are you okay?" she asks. "You were yelling, crying out."

"Too bright, too bright." My overhead lamp shines in my face, blinding me all over again.

She holds back her tears. "Frank, you were yelling her name."

She says, "Shhhh, Frank, it's okay," like I'm a baby, until my eyes are closed and she thinks I'm asleep. "That's right," she soothes, "relax, Frankie, relax. My poor boy." She turns the light off, closes the door, and walks away.

I look into the space and try to reclaim Meredith's hand on my thigh. Thigh, wake up. You were touched. Amputees feel old limbs. Why can't I feel a dead girl's touch? I try again. Her hand. On my skin. Her hair. On me. Her body. Where is it?

I am still awake when my father gets home. Maybe they will share a drink. Maybe they will really talk.

Mom says, clear as a bell, "He will never stop dreaming about her."

Neither of my parents can say her name. When they refer to the accident, they use mostly pronouns: *she, her*, sometimes *his girlfriend*. Once, Mom called her *that bitch*.

My father speaks slowly. He says something unintelligible, maybe, "That's the least of his problems." He talks too loud. He is obviously drunk. It's too late at night for him to be anything else. I wonder if he thinks about my accident before he gets behind the wheel after downing a few. Weird, if he doesn't.

"I am tired," my mother says.

My father says nothing.

"I am tired," she repeats. "He is so heavy. I barely got him into the bed tonight. He is so . . ." Silence. Dead silence. Fill in the blank:

Pathetic.

Helpless.

Useless.

My mother cries. "You should see what they're saying about him. Everywhere . . . first it was the TV, then the radio. Today I read something about him on that damn computer." Silence. Steps. Up and down. "It's never going to stop. They will never forgive him. All these people . . . they want him to go to jail. Or worse. They talk about her like she was some kind of saint."

"You have to stop reading that shit, Rosemary," my father says. "What do we care what those losers think about Frank? The talk will die down. It always does. His case did not set a precedent. Leave it be."

"He was supposed to go to college. He had everything to look forward to." Her voice goes up an octave. "She was a slut."

"Rosemary, it was an accident. A terrible tragedy."

That's what Judge Martin O'Connor said, too. "This is a terrible tragedy." Google him and find the link that tells you all about His Honor and the many important decisions he's made.

All of the pertinent information regarding my case is in a benevolent-decisions file.

I had just been transferred to rehab. Meredith's parents were begging the judge to do something, anything, please. They were quoted in the paper: "Frank Marder is guilty of vehicular manslaughter, driving while intoxicated. His Honor can't ignore two dead bodies. He may be injured, but he's still alive. His Honor must know she was our only daughter."

My dad's lawyer approached the Steins with tender looks and long handshakes. For two weeks, he filmed my rehab, documented my schedule of care. We viewed it together: the judge, the Steins, my parents and me, and Drock. I stared at myself being moved and stretched and cleaned. That was me. My body. My arms and legs, moving through space. I opened and closed my eyes, the way you watch a slasher film, waiting for the gory parts to be over.

The ruling took place on a Monday, Judge's usual day off. We gathered in the patient lounge. "That is the most fucked-up thing I've ever heard of," Freeberg said. "There's no fuckin way they are putting you away." He popped a wheelie. "You aren't going to hurt nothing never again. You are already in jail."

Chad Downey, my lawyer, wore an old suit and a shirt with a butter stain on the collar. His papers were overflowing; when he went through them, he dropped the whole mess on the floor. "I'm sorry, Your Honor," he said. Meredith's family lawyer was just the opposite: organized and professionally dressed, with fire-engine-red hair and a conservative black suit that Meredith would have loathed. Judge stood between them in a long black robe.

I wondered what he had on underneath. Tennis clothes? Pajamas? Nothing at all?

A lady in the corner set up a laptop and took notes. Judge Martin O'Connor banged his gavel on the snack table. "These are extraordinary circumstances, and for that reason, I'll hear arguments." It took hours. He looked, he asked questions, he talked to the therapists. He investigated every aspect of my sorry life before declaring me "punished well beyond the statute of the law." I was sure Meredith's dad was going to spontaneously combust, but the judge wouldn't hear any of it. Judge Martin O'Connor banged his gavel one more time and proclaimed that my disability would forever be a reminder to people that justice was real. "Society, Mr. and Mrs. Stein, is better off having this boy in their midst as a living reminder of what can happen when you do something as stupid as drive while intoxicated." He issued a similar statement to the press. "When people see Frank Marder, they will remember that carelessness kills. They will be reminded not to drink and drive. They will look at him and understand, this is what can happen if you do."

I would have laughed, except it was my life they were talking about. My life. I was the living reminder.

"You have to calm down," Dad says. I wonder what time it is, if they will talk in the kitchen until the sun comes up. "Just relax," he says. He doesn't sound relaxed. Neither of them sounds happy to be up together in the middle of the night.

I stare into the blackness. She is not going to relax.

"You never help." Her voice is too loud.

"I do my part." His voice is loud, too, but under control—insult induced sobriety.

"Sure, you do, Hal. Sure you help." Shrill. Each sentence a step higher. "You do the light stuff. The clean stuff. When was the last time you fed our son? When was the last time you cleaned out his ass?"

"Rosemary, baby—" I know what's coming next.

"Don't, Hal."

"Baby." Silence. "Baby, baby, baby."

"Bastard."

And with that, tonight's version of The Baby and Bastard Show officially begins. Usually, they fight about sex and love or what's for dinner, but tonight it's all about me.

"I need some help. We need to hire that nurse."

And the money.

"I can't do it myself."

And how they're never going to have enough.

"You have to. We can't afford—"

"Why not?"

"It's been two weeks, Rosemary. It will get easier."

"We need to get that nurse. I can't do it alone. We can take out another—"

"No we can't!" he shouts. "No more debt. We can't handle it. We need to preserve the resources we have left."

I stare into the darkness. *Kill me,* I want to shout, *if you don't want to take care of me.* Kill me. Stop fighting and put us all out of our misery.

"You ignore him."

"I have to make a living."

"You have to make time for your girlfriend. Don't think I don't smell her every time you walk in the door."

"That's not fair."

"What's not fair is that I am working my ass off, and your life hasn't changed at all."

I wonder what the Steins fight about. Meredith thought they had a good marriage. She thought they were faithful.

Something shatters. Their voices blend together.

"You don't love him."

"You don't love *me.*"

The blackness hugs my face. Except for my pillow, I don't have a landmark. I really don't know where I am.

"You know, they're doing research," she says.

My father laughs. "You mean that article about the computer chip that they want to plant in someone's brain? Baby, that's years away."

She sobs.

"What do you want from me?" He runs up the steps to their bedroom overhead. "What do you want me to do?"

The blackness is crushing me.

"Baby, let's face it." But no, she can't face it.

She yells, "Bastard!" And he yells, "Shut up!" and he's opening drawers, banging doors, stamping his feet. Back and forth. Across the room.

"You can't face anything."

"You don't do anything."

Dead. I should be dead. I should be in the ground, and they should be going to work and eating dinners and not fighting about nurses and gossip and money.

"Look at him, Rosemary, and tell me right now: if that's what he's going to be, what's the fucking difference?"

Another crash. Another cry. My father's heavy steps out the door. What if he leaves for good? What will my mother do? She should be quiet, let him have his nights out. He's not a perfect man, but we need him. Until I really am dead, we need him.

"Are you awake?" my mother asks.

"I hate when you fight." No reason to pretend I haven't heard every word. "Can you turn on the light? And roll me to the side? My water—"

She holds the straw to my lips. Too guilty to ignore the command of the invalid.

But not too guilty to ask questions. "What does it feel like?" she asks. "Not to feel your body?"

What does it feel like? "It *feels* like nothing. It isn't the same as floating. I know I'm not weightless, but I don't feel anything either." She sits on the bed and rubs my head hard and sings me a lullaby from my childhood. The tips of her fingers push on my temples.

"I remember when you were a little boy, you used to love to have your head rubbed. You were like a puppy. Every night, you begged us to rub your head." She rubs some more, now through tears. "How could you do it, Frank? How could you get in that car?"

It doesn't matter. I got in the car. I wanted the girl. I met her. I liked her. I wanted her day and night.

I drove to Meredith's house, a large white house with black shutters and a red door. The garden was overgrown; the welcome mat said, *Paws.* I rang the doorbell, eye to eye with a silver hand that said, *Follow my commandments and be holy.*

I looked up at the star-filled sky. I prayed she was as wild as she claimed to be. I prayed her parents were out; I didn't want to have to waste even five minutes being polite.

Meredith opened the door and took one, two, three giant steps into me. "Perfect timing." She kissed me with both hands on my shoulders; she didn't flinch when mine slid to her ass. For that moment, I believed in God. She smiled this crooked, sexy smile.

She gave directions. Left. Right. Straight through town. Through a neighborhood where the streets have names like Quail Ridge and Pheasant Avenue, and the houses are coordinated in shape and color.

This one was one of the yellow ones.

A large guy with jet black hair and a Marauders Varsity cap opened the door. He grabbed Meredith behind the neck, and she punched him in the gut. "This is Frank," she said. "Frank, Paul." You could tell he liked her. You could tell he wanted to be me.

I stood up straighter. He extended his hand. "Paul Rogers." We shook like boxers in the ring. "Hey, I know you." He crossed his arms over his puffed-up chest. "We played on the same Little League team in third grade."

My last year of organized ball. A season I'd like to forget.

Meredith didn't wait for me to trip over my words. She squeezed my hand and pulled me past Paul, into the party. The refrigerator was stocked. I grabbed a beer and a corner spot on the already-crowded couch.

The playoffs were in full swing. Pizzas covered the tables. A keg sat in the corner. Music blared; two couples were dancing in the corner, slow dancing to fast, loud music. It was a good night to be in a house with a girl and a beer and a bigscreen TV.

The pitcher was on his game. It was a tight series. I reached behind Meredith and sank deep into the couch. We were watching and touching and people all around us were talking and laughing.

After three innings, I realized I didn't know the score. Her hand was on my thigh, getting closer to the crease near my crotch. I didn't care who was batting what and who had dropped balls. She was touching me—in public—and I didn't even have to say, "I love you."

But right then, I almost did; I almost said it, that is. She was going to be my first.

I never told her I was a virgin.

I never told her that I was planning to leave for college and never come back.

I never told her that I was not interested in having a long-term relationship, and she never asked. We were together for the "now," for having a great time before going off to live our real lives. Those were the rules. I wasn't the only one who wanted to have sex and fun and wild times but nothing personal.

She was ready to take some risks, too.

We didn't have sex the night of the party. Instead, we waited for the next night. My parents had plans. We were alone in the house.

"So, what do you like best about sex?" she asked from the corner of my room. We were sipping gin-and-tonics and eating smoked cheddar cheese on little square crackers. I took another bite and another sip and hoped that Meredith would forget about talking and get into my bed. We had three hours, max. If we hurried up, we could do it twice.

But Meredith wasn't budging until she had my answer. I pretended to think. "Um . . . I don't know. What do I like best about sex? What kind of question is that? Why don't we just go to bed?"

This was not acceptable. She grabbed my hands and looked me in the eye. Her eyes were almost black in the dim light. "No, really," she said. "Tell me. What do you like best?"

"Um . . . anything." Lame answer, but true. Anything would be great. Anything before I explode.

She bounced on the bed and pulled me down next to her. We wrestled a little, laughing, trying to figure out how we fit. "Anything, anything?" she asked. She had her hands on my neck, on my back, unzipping my fly, all at one time, I still don't know how. "Come on, Frank Marder." She grabbed my shirt and pulled me on top of her. "You can do better than that."

I laughed it off, groped for her sweater; she pushed my hands away, then got off the bed and took it off herself.

The radio played old eighties music, bad-dancing music; my bed smelled like cherry and grape. We were halfway to naked. I pulled her toward me and kissed her again, touching by accident, fumbling to see if we were both ready.

I was.

She seemed to be.

I put my hands on her hips and willed myself to reach in, to reach under, to explore.

But she wouldn't stop talking. "Frank," she said, flipping me on my back, "do you understand what we are about to do?" She tickled my neck and nibbled my left ear.

I hoped so. There was no way I misunderstood, was there?

She stayed on top of me and we kissed. Her face felt hot and soft and almost wet. "You'll never lie in this bed without thinking of me."

She threw my jeans on the floor and undressed in spurts, each piece of clothing to its own corner. Skirt to the left, T-shirt to the back. She stared right at me as she unsnapped her lacy black bra. I pinched her nipples, and she arched like a cat. Smiling. Playing with my hair. "You know, my friend, you will not be able to have sex with anyone in this bed without thinking about me."

So? I thought. So what. So I think of her. How bad can that be?

I was living my fantasy, her breath on my neck, my hands on her body. Up and down. She took my hand and gave me a tour. "Touch here. Like this." She was soft and her skin tasted like milk. She said I was salty. Like a pretzel on a hot day in the park. We fiddled and wrestled and finally, she said, "Okay."

She let me in and then it went fast. Fast, fast, fast, in-and-out fast, uncontrollable-fast—start to finish—no screams, no *oh my gods*, no promises of love. She kept looking at me. Eye to eye. She smiled when I whispered, "Oh," and finished. If it wasn't right, she didn't tell me. She didn't look upset when I woke her up and told her that we should get dressed.

Before I dropped her off, we made plans for the week. The month. My mother had one meeting that week; the next week, two. We spoke quietly, one word at a time: *yes, no, sure, okay, great.*

I couldn't have known that she would be my first and my last, that in one month, someone would carry her body from the street to the ambulance to the morgue, that her lips and her hands would be the only ones I would ever feel. I was thinking about flesh and sex and my own naked body. I was thinking of all the women who would follow Meredith. I was thinking, *Thank you, thank you, thank you, thank you.*

We slept together three times after that, four times altogether. Four.

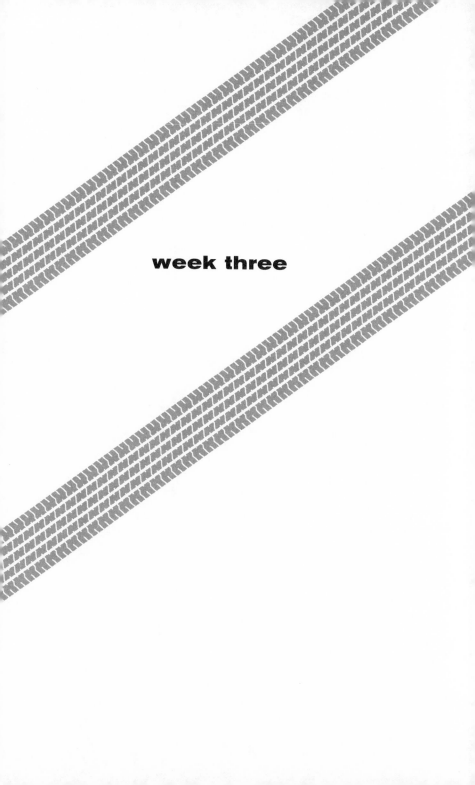

week three

Sunset decides that it is time to take me into town to begin navigating what she calls the real world. "Your mom is going to spend the day with her friends. We are going to get on out of here, Frank, and begin to relearn your environment."

I knew the drill. Motor down the sidewalk at a constant speed. Slow down for the cutouts. Speed up for the bumps. Wait for my "body" to open doors. "I already know what to do."

Mom kisses my head on her way out the door. She wears jeans and a striped oxford shirt. Perfume. A headband. She tries to suppress a smile, but anyone can see she's pumped. Her cheeks are flushed pink. "I'm going to have lunch with the girls." First time since I've been home.

"Have a great time," Sunset says, shooing her out the door. She puts on her jacket. "Today we'll meet Victoria and take a short stroll down Main Street. Maybe more. Let's see how it goes."

"Could you lose the body talk?"

She looks confused.

"I don't stroll, walk, or meander. I roll. Motor. Advance."

"So sensitive all of a sudden." She smiles, but I can tell she feels self-conscious about her mistake. "You tell me if you want to stop anywhere." She likes to act as if we are friends and she isn't getting paid and this isn't a therapeutic assignment and we are spending time together for fun.

Fun. What is that?

Sunset drives the new gimp-mobile to town, and I exit the oversized door without too much trouble.

The air is cold on my face. I close my eyes against the wind. "The first time out can be very overwhelming." Sunset must think I'm crying.

Victoria is waiting on the corner. "Use your chin to get started down the sidewalk," she says as if I have some other body part at my disposal.

For a moment, it seems easy. I can do it. I travel two, maybe three squares, and then some guy in jeans and a puffy coat tells us to stop. "Shouldn't you be controlling the chair?" he asks Victoria. Not me.

He won't even look at me.

I have a list of things I'd like to say, but Sunset gives me the eye. *He doesn't get it.*

"No, I shouldn't be. Frank can drive his chair independently." Her glare is more condemning than anything I'd have the nerve to dole out.

The guy shakes his head. He's not up for a lesson. "Sorry for asking." I put my chin in first gear and immediately roll over a bump.

"What was that?" I'm sure I've just run over the jerk's foot. A bump could be anything—a kid, a box of Milk Duds, a bottle— how would I know? I can't see my wheels. Maybe the guy's right.

Victoria shakes her head, like she knows what I'm thinking. "No biggie. It was just a heave in the sidewalk."

She reminds me how to control the speed of my chair, probably for the benefit of our inquisitor, who is still lurking somewhere, I'm sure. "Your tires have traction, and you have a good motor. It's other people's responsibility to get out of the way."

Yeah. His responsibility. We continue, and I hit another bump. This one I'm ready for. I tripped on it six years ago and chipped a tooth, back when the storefront was called Tried and Trendy. Now it's a Gap. Mom nearly had a fit when I got home. Her baby's beautiful face! How could you be so careless?

I hit another bump, a smaller one, then another. How come this town can't fix the sidewalk? Don't they realize how hard it is to deal with this shit?

Victoria shows me how to maneuver over the curb. I concentrate on my chin and for a second, forget about the crowd. There are a lot of people in town, everywhere but near us. In front of us, people walk shoulder to shoulder. I bet a million dollars they do the same behind us. But around us, there is space. Air and room. People are moving out of our path, making sure to avoid us. I consider shouting, "I'm not contagious. Look at me."

Most people, as they pass us, look away. They don't make eye contact with the crip. Too confrontational. A few sneak a peek, check me out. Some shake their heads in pity; some can't help rubbing their necks. Two crotch checks—and counting. The smart few, the ones who read the paper and watch the news, look twice. *Oh, yes. That must be Frank Marder. The boy who killed the girl, who killed the man, and broke his own neck.* The moment of recognition is easy to spot.

If Walking Frank had seen someone in a chair, he would have done exactly the same thing.

On the next corner, one of my father's old friends is walking toward us. He hasn't been to the house since I got home. Dad used to play cards with him. Squash, too. I prepare myself for our greetings, his apologies, his guilty comments. Sunset and Victoria flank the chair; he can't avoid me. The street is crowded. He is not getting by. He catches my eye—there is no escape.

And then, he's gone. He makes a left down the side street and disappears without saying hello, good-bye, or even *How the hell are you, Frank. How's the old man?*

We part the crowd. Two girls stare and shake their heads. One wipes away a tear, for Meredith, no doubt.

I wonder what they think they see. Meredith-killer, head, loser, freak, wheelchair, murderer. Victim? Ha!

My chair won't move. "Curb," Sunset says. She pushes me into the street. "They have to make better cutouts."

"Let's go home." The world doesn't want to see me; they don't want to be reminded on Main Street that Meredith is dead, buried, six feet under; that their own children are risk takers.

I hit another bump and some guy jumps back out of the way. As we pass each other, he spits on the ground. Maybe it's a coincidence, maybe not. I almost lose it. "I can't do it."

Sunset stands in front of me. "You can do it. Look straight ahead. Memorize where you are. Tell me when you need help. Take charge." Out of the blue, she says, "There are no fairy-tale endings, Frank. Just hard work."

We keep going. This is my downtown, my neighborhood. Not all these people hate me. Sunset runs into an old friend. "Pull over," she says. "Take five." The three of them reminisce.

Murphy's Law: you will always see the very people you want to avoid on your first day out. Mine are just ahead. Harry and Jocelyn, arm in arm, walking and laughing, are headed in my direction. She throws her hair back. He drapes his arm on her shoulder. They don't see me.

"Sunset." I try hard to smile, but my eyes feel heavy, and she won't stop talking to her friend. My smile is so forced that it turns to stone.

"Sunset." I try to get her attention, but she's midstory, and the three of them are laughing.

"Sunset."

She finally looks. "Are you cold?"

"Let's go," I say. "Now."

Harry and Jocelyn stop in front of the chair.

Too late.

"Hi, Frank." At the sound of my name, Sunset and Victoria flank the chair. They introduce themselves, then step to the side to continue their conversation.

"How are you?" Harry asks. His hair is trim. He is not wearing anything with a Yankees logo.

"Fine."

"You look good."

"Thanks. You, too." We sound like old ladies.

Jocelyn fiddles with her bracelet. She adjusts the collar of her jacket.

"Hi, Jocelyn," I say. "How's it going?"

"Okay."

She and Harry drop their arms. They stand side by side, staring at me. Jocelyn elbows him. "Great, really. I got into Skidmore. Early decision."

Harry's face remains blank.

"What about you?" I ask. "Have you heard?"

"Yeah," Harry says. Long pause. "I'm going to Ithaca." He steps to the side.

"Not Vassar?" I ask. It was always Vassar. Vassar and NYU. Or Vassar and Bucknell. Or Lehigh. I try not to sound surprised.

"I wish we had some snow," Jocelyn says. "We always have snow by now."

"Yeah. It's weird," Harry says. "I can't remember the last time it was this warm."

Even weather talk is difficult.

Sunset and Victoria return. "I'll give you a call, Harry. I got a voice-activated phone. Soon."

Jocelyn stares at my chair. He looks at a piece of blue sky. "Okay. Sounds like a plan." Together, they walk away.

He was not the one who pushed *me* away.

As we motor along, I half expect him to charge up behind me. Yell. Call me a *putz*, the way he used to when we fought. Or apologize for not calling, for being a body, for having a girlfriend. What do they call it . . . survivor's guilt? Why doesn't he have it? Why doesn't he feel how hard this is for me?

But, instead, he says nothing. He has moved on.

Sunset won't take me home, even when I beg.

"Not yet, bud," she says. "I'm starved." Sunset motions to me to make a left down a quiet side street. "Let's go get some lunch."

Victoria shakes her head. "No can do," she says. "I gotta bolt. I have another patient." She scrunches her nose. "Stroke, diabetic. He's a whiner. All he does is complain. Not like you, Frank." She winks.

It's a setup.

"I want to go home." She can't possibly want to feed me in public.

"Sorry. You need to get used to people looking at you, and people need to get used to seeing people like you out and about," Sunset says.

"Sounds like a lousy idea."

"Sounds like a great idea. Don't you think your mother would like to get out now and again?"

Duh. "Okay," I say. "Feed me."

Sunset smiles. "Great. Let's go to Mike's."

Mike's.

My favorite hangout.

She's lost it. At Mike's, the aisles are narrow and the tables are undersized, and I've never walked in there without recognizing half a dozen people. "I don't want to go to Mike's." I want to go to a fast-food restaurant with take-out service and wheelchair-accessible aisles—preferably in the next town, where no one will know me, and we don't have to worry about running into any more former best friends.

Sunset shakes her head. "We're going to Mike's. Your mother told me it was your favorite place. I heard all about your cheesecake fetish and how you like your potatoes crisp." She smiles. "Besides, they are expecting us. I called ahead. They're holding the big table. Don't worry."

Great. Thanks, Sunset. Can't wait.

Sunset has to tip my chair way back to manage the big step up into the front door. In the foyer, a million Mikes greet us. Every wall is covered with pictures of Mike the First with famous people who loved his cooking: Jimmy Durante, Frank Sinatra, Sammy Davis Junior, and even President Kennedy. Mike is always standing front and center, facing the camera, chest out, big smile, cigarette in one hand, the other arm around the star. All the pictures, even the new ones, featuring today's Mike—a big, burly guy with jet-black hair—are in black and white, and they're all signed, *Whenever I come to New England, I eat at Mike's.*

There are banners at the front counter. Trophies, too. *Mooretown's Culinary Landmark for 40 years. Voted First in the Region: Best Breakfast.*

Mike himself jogs to the door. Patty, the head waitress, follows on his heels, and together, they usher us in.

"Hi, Frank. Good to see you," Patty says. She puts her arms on my arms in a pseudo-embrace. "I've been serving him eggs, bacon, and home fries since he was a boy." Sunset nods.

"She gave me my first Pokemon cards," I add.

Together we move into the restaurant. Even though it isn't as crowded as it could be, there are enough people here to notice that the room is suddenly silent. "Sit down right over there," Mike says. Patty slaps him.

"It's okay," I say. I like Patty and Mike.

We follow her down the aisle to the empty corner table. People avoid making eye contact. They look at their eggs and potatoes, their pancakes and sandwiches as I motor past.

One little boy stands up in his seat and looks right at me. "Can I have a ride?" he asks. His mother yanks his arm and sits him back in the booth. "Shhh," she says. "Don't be rude."

"Let's get out of here," I whisper to Sunset.

She sits down and opens the menu. "What did you say was good?"

"It's too hard."

"Should I get pancakes?"

"I want to leave."

"So go. I'm staying."

"You know I . . ."

I don't say "can't," because Patty arrives.

"What'll it be?" Patty looks at my motionless hands. I can tell she is trying to figure out exactly how I'm going to eat.

"Pancakes," Sunset says. "With a side order of fruit."

"The usual," I say. The big breakfast. Eggs, cakes, potatoes, and sausage. If I'm going to be humiliated, I might as well get the works.

The food arrives in record time. Sunset doesn't have to ask for a refill of coffee. It just comes. Need more jelly? Syrup? Butter? Patty has never been faster.

"Great service," Sunset says. "I had heard they were slow."

"They usually are slow." Earth to Sunset: They want us out of here. They want people to eat, not stare at the freak show.

She spoons the food into my mouth in small bites, in equal proportions, so I get egg and sausage, alternating with potato and pancake, in every bite.

The boy who wanted the ride stops by. "Can't you feed yourself yet? I can tie my shoes. Are you in special ed?"

Before I can think of an answer, his mother jerks him away, nearly dislocating his arm. "Sorry," she says to Sunset.

"That's okay," I tell her back.

We are almost done when an old man approaches our table. He places a pamphlet on my lap. "It's God's world," he says, his eyes slightly glazed. "Not man's. *God's.*" And he walks away.

"That guy is a nut job," Sunset says, shaking her head. She puts a twenty on the table as he walks back down the aisle. "Crazy."

I hope so.

I used to think about God the same way I thought about those public service announcements you see all the time on TV. *This is a test. This is only a test.* If this was a real emergency, you would be directed to do something or other, but nobody does, because that long chime is ringing, and we turn the volume down or go into the next room for a Coke.

Know what I mean?

God was a cheap construction made up by people like my mother who were just waiting for an emergency that was never going to come. I never bought the creation thing, the parting of the seas, the water into wine. Science made a lot more sense. Laws over rituals. Rules over ethics.

Funny, now that I could use a miracle, I see how right I was, how absolutely ridiculous the notion is.

In the hospital, Mom had a whole bunch of church buddies who came and prayed with her. They made an assembly line of prayer so that every minute of the day, God was getting a message for Frank.

Do they think that one more prayer would have done it? Was there a buzzer that went off too fast? If so, why did they give up?

If there really was a God, there'd have to be a "life mulligan"— a holy do-over. You could use it only once, so you'd have to save it for a really important moment. Like when you are driving on a side street and you've forgotten to turn on your lights, and your girl is holding onto you, and you can't think of anything else.

Then you could use it. Or even better, you could wait until you feel the car swerve, and hear the thud and the smack. Then, right before your girlfriend's life ended, you could shout, "Life mulligan!" and it would all go back to normal. No one would die. No one would end up in the hospital. No one's neck would break in two.

The Steins are Jewish. They buried Meredith thirty-one hours after she died.

"Do you believe this is God's world?" I ask Sunset, to keep the conversation going. Suddenly, I'm not so anxious to go home.

"I don't believe in organized religion," Sunset says, like I couldn't have predicted that a mile away. "I do believe in community. In people helping each other." She looks at the pamphlet the old man left. "All this bullshit is just there to make us less scared. But really, we should focus on what we can do here."

"So you don't think I deserve this? That God is teaching me some sort of lesson?"

"No. I don't. I think you got the raw end of a deal, Frank. What happened to you sucks. I hope that science is going to come up with something big for you someday. I really do."

We sit in silence. It feels good to hear someone say it. It sucks. Being a head sucks.

"Do you know who Christopher Reeve was?" she asks.

"The guy in the old Superman movies. The therapists at the hospital told me about him."

"He fell off his horse and broke his neck. Sustained a high cervical injury. But he never gave up. He worked for people like you the rest of his life. He raised money and awareness. He worked out like a maniac. You should look him up on the Net. His story might inspire you. He learned to move his little finger."

His little finger. I want to cry.

"He's dead, isn't he?"

Sunset nods, stands up, and adjusts my joystick into the on position. "Yeah," Sunset says. "He died. We all die someday."

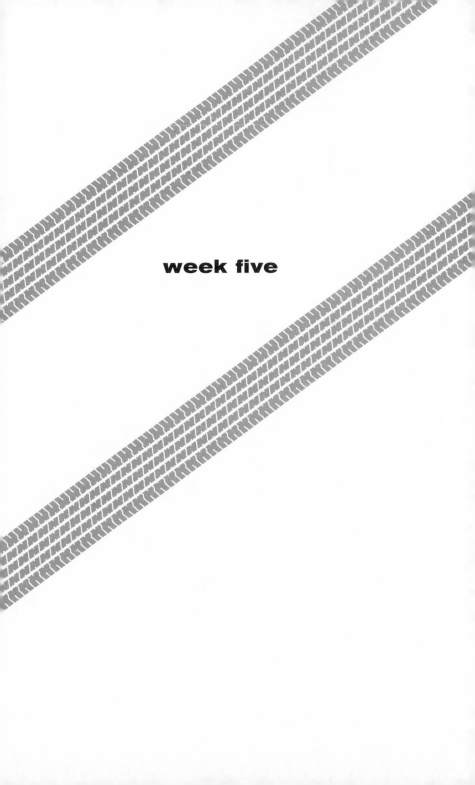

week five

Believe it or not, there are still people who want to talk about me. Today, *www.Quadkingonthenet.com* continues to retrace my day in town. You can hear about my meal, what I ate, even what Sunset and I talked about. I'm pissed at Patty; she's the last person I expected to post.

> **Serveseggs:** I wanted to give him a bib, but they started talking about God, so I didn't.

> **econboy889:** I saw FM F2F. I was going to give him the finger, but when I got up close, he looked totally pathetic. He uses HIS CHIN to move his chair. I'd rather be dead.

> **Serveseggs:** He can't feed himself either. All he did was talk, open his mouth and chew.

> **Anonymous:** This town makes me sick. All you people need to find something else to talk about. Frank Marder needs to figure out a way to live. We should be kind to him.

> **Rowergirl:** FFW! He shouldn't be allowed 2 go out. IIMAD2U, there are people who are doing experiments on jerks like him. They're making computer chips to put in the brain. He could walk again. It makes me want to puke.

> **econboy889:** Rowergirl: R U busy 2 nite? LMIRL!

"Frank, we're late." My mother stands next to me at the computer, and for a moment reads with me. "Who do you think Anonymous is?"

"It's not you?" I ask.

She laughs. "No. Sorry. Maybe it's Harry." Her mouth turns serious. "You really should call him." She shoots me a maternal look and checks her watch. "Turn it off. We have to be at the hospital in half an hour."

I secretly bet myself an arm and a leg that someone from the hospital will post my checkup results.

"They want to see how we're doing. You never know, honey," she says. She hasn't lost hope. "They might want to accelerate your physical therapy."

Maybe Anonymous is Harry. Harry is the kind of guy to do that. Stick up for me, even though we're not talking. Maybe she's right; I should call him, tell him to come over, that I'm done being an asshole. Or maybe not. Maybe the best thing I can do for my friend is forget him.

I make a decision, and then *bam*, it all feels wrong.

I miss Harry. I need to apologize.

There's no place like home, no place like home. The rehab wing of the hospital looks exactly the same. Nurses peek out of rooms and behind counters to say hello to me. There are no people looking around me, wondering about me; these are not the people who write about me in their spare time.

Zoe jogs over and tousles my hair. "Hey, Frank, looking good."

I wish I could wave; I wish I could shake her hand. She would freak out!

My mother gives her a big embrace. A few other nurses see us and come over to say hello, too. Mom clutches her purse with both hands. "How are you?" she asks each nurse. "So nice to see you." Zoe squeezes her hands, yes, yes, everything is great, my life is great, work is fine, yes, yes, it is nice to see you, too.

The crowd is breaking up when Cecilia emerges. She breaks into a run and almost falls into my lap; she stops herself just in time. She squeezes my neck with her tiny warm hands and smiles just the way she did every day that I was here. "Frank! Anything to report on this fine and most magnificent day?"

"I knew you'd say that!"

She takes a step back, like I'm a piece of art to admire. Then she closes in for a big hug. Strange, her scent has changed; now she smells like tropical fruit. Her hair looks pretty today, too: smooth, no kinks, and her teeth don't seem so big or yellow. She thrusts her hand in my face.

"The doctor will—"

"Not the nails, Frank. Look at my finger. My ring finger."

I smile. "So, Dr. Love finally popped the question?" I ask.

She nods, waves the diamond in Mom's face, and jumps up and down. "Last week," she says, "at Serendipity."

"Congratulations."

Life goes on. One month ago, Cecilia was single, she was tacky, she talked too loud, smiled too much. Now she looks lovely. She is happy, grown up, moving on with her life. I am not different, I have not changed, I am frozen in time and space.

"You look great," she says. "In for a checkup?"

"Drock," I say, smiling. "Here to see the man."

"Good luck," she says, on her feet and moving away faster than I can roll. She waves. She's got a whole new set of paralyzed guys in need. "You should stop in 103 and see Richard."

"Richard?"

"Freeberg," she says, like I should know something. "He's back."

Freeberg isn't just back, he's a complete C7. Not a whole lot better than me.

He doesn't look surprised when I motor into the room. He just stares at me, chair to chair, quad to quad. He manages a flick of the wrist. Yeah, he's still on top.

"Who told you?" he asks.

"Cecilia. I came in for a checkup. I didn't know."

He says nothing.

"What happened?"

"They dragged their asses on that car. Every time I called, they said the same thing: any day, man, any day. Yeah, sure. I figured I was never going to get it." He looks past me to the clock. "I took matters into my own hands."

He stares at his limp hands. I stare at them, too. He had hands. He had working hands and a working dick—practically an entire working body. But now he doesn't.

"Took out my dad's old Firebird. Used my cane to work the clutch. It was going great. But then I messed up and smashed into a tree. I didn't think . . ."

"Were you trying to . . ." I don't finish. Heads talk a lot about death—how can you not? It's the only way out. I can't pretend I haven't thought about it, but I never go further. I never ask . . . except . . . What I did to Harry stinks. There's no excuse. I should have apologized.

"Nah," he says. "I didn't want to off myself. I was just having fun." He starts crying. "Just wanted to take a drive, feel like a man." He shrugs.

A guy with a helmet raps on the door as he walks down the hall singing "New York, New York" at the top of his lungs.

"Who's that?" I ask.

"Vincent Orifice."

"'Orifice,' as in . . ."

"Yeah. I call him 'The Hole.'" Freeberg smirks. "My new best bud. Guy was a rapist, convicted. He was going away, too. The whole thing went down while we were in here." He shakes his head. "Guy was the worst kind. Raped his own kid. Got eight to twelve."

"That seems light."

Freeberg rolls closer. "His old lady thought so, too. Said that the judge took pity on him 'cause he said he was abused. After his sentencing, she pulled a gun. Shot him in the head." Freeberg looks like he's gaining some of his spark back, but I feel sick.

"Apparently, they swept up half his gray matter off the court-room floor." He chuckles. "The guy comes here, spends some time in a coma. Then he wakes up and bam—he's a goddamn diva. Every day he walks up and down the hall, singing. Even plays the piano sometimes. Sings all . . ." I think he's going to say, "fuckin day," but he doesn't. "The guy sings all day. He doesn't remember his wife, the kid he raped, or anything else, for that matter. All he cares about is the music."

He chuckles. I can't help looking at his hands again. His hands. Freeberg says, "You gotta wonder. It's like he was destined to go bad. What if his name had been Rogers or Smith or even something like Rosenhorn . . ." He laughs. "Then maybe he wouldn't have turned out so bad. He might not have raped the girl. He might have been a stockbroker or a doctor or a janitor. He might have been a great man."

I nod. "But what chance did he have with a name like Orifice?" It's hard not to snicker.

"Actually, it's pronounced, Or-i-fee-kee," Freeberg says, and we both laugh harder than we should. Considering.

"Really, *Marder*, what chance does a guy like that have?"

We listen to him walk back down the hall toward us, this time singing Aretha Franklin. "He has no idea. Before he got shot, his life was a wreck. Now he's so happy. How'd he get so damn lucky?"

Zoe the nurse comes in. "You're late," she says. No smile. No jokes. They are definitely not kissing in the back room anymore. He swipes his face with his shoulder and rolls slowly out the door. Real slow, without bravado. No wheelie.

He pivots and smiles weakly. "I don't really remember what I wanted so bad. I don't know why I thought I could get away with anything again. I really . . ."

Fucked up.

I don't know what to say. Freeberg doesn't need to hear it from me.

My mother finds me and puts her hand on my cheek, wipes away my tears. "I'm sorry," she says.

I was so jealous of him. I wanted what he had. But I don't gloat now. We squander chances; we miss opportunities. The Hole makes his way down the hall. *"Don't let the sun go down on me."*

I follow my mother to the doctor's office.

Drock checks me up and down. He stands in front of my wheelchair and pats my head like I am a dog who understands the commands *here* and *sit*.

"You know, Frank, there are a lot of people with quadriplegia who get some return, sometimes a whole level."

"Yes, I know. Victoria tells me that every time I see her." I think, why not me? Why am I still waiting?

"How's the therapy? How's Sunset?" He stands back while a young Asian man pokes me and shifts me, pulls me forward out of my chair. "We're going to lift up your shirt and pull down your pants. Take a look down there." He hums The Hole's last tune, but his tone is pitchy, off-key.

The Asian guy says, "I'm going to test your sensation. Tell me if you feel anything at all."

Presumably he's touching me somewhere.

He moves my arms, my legs. *Tap, tap, tap.* Been there, done that. No improvement.

"Hey, your skin sure looks nice," he says. He puts me back in the chair. Then Drock himself pokes my belly. He shows the Asian guy something. They nod. They make small doctor sounds, but they do not talk—not to me.

His finger goes in and out, in and out. Do it all you want, Drock.

"Gotta little paunch there, Frank."

We think we're done, but we're not. Drock looks behind him to the door, and Stacey appears. "Frank, do you remember

Stacey?"

I nod. Yes, streaky Stacey, the flirt, PT, great ass. She walks in and I can't help looking head to toe.

She is all dressed up. Like a professional.

"Well, Frank, recently, Stacey was awarded a grant."

Stacey corrects her posture. I check out Drock's hand. No more ring. Not even a shadow of a ring. She takes two steps away from him. I wonder what that means. "Would you like to hear about it?" she asks.

"Uh-huh." Sure. What the hell. You're looking good. I'm here. Got the time. Let's do it.

Drock pipes in. "Stacey is going to go to area high schools to talk to students about head and spinal cord injuries." He smiles at her, and she looks away. "And how to prevent them. We all feel like you would be an excellent candidate to help out." He rubs his stubbly pepper-and-salt chin like he's thinking about something. Maybe her. Maybe someone else.

"Frank, we are hoping that you will go with Stacey into the schools and talk about your life since your injury."

Stacey jumps in. "We know you haven't been home long, but I'm willing to wait until you are ready. You are everything we are looking for: smart, articulate—"

"A head," I add.

"Person with quadriplegia." She looks a little uncomfortable. "Frank, the candidate must be able to speak in front of large groups. You were the captain of the debate team. You could do it." I wait, expecting her to say please. *Pretty please, Frank, with sugar on top, please be my official head for a day.*

Drock closes the gap and squeezes Stacey's shoulder; she

takes another large step away. He doesn't flinch. "I can find someone else to do it. No problem," he says. "It won't change anything. You will still be paralyzed. Kids will still do stupid things. But maybe this happened to you so that you can do it. Maybe this is a way you could find meaning for your life."

I look at my mom. She is nodding almost ferociously, *yes, yes, Frank, make a difference in someone's life. Do something for someone else. Make me proud.*

I should do it, just say yes, do the right thing, but I can't. They want me to get up on a stage and talk about the most intimate, depressing details of my life. Putting me on display. Using me.

I say, "I'll think about it."

When I get home, I send Harry a message. Chickenshit e-mail.

Quadking: Hey! WU? R U anonymous? Can I apologize?

His return comes minutes later. At least some things haven't changed—Harry spends a lot of time at his computer.

Harrycarry: I'm not *anonymous.* I don't want to talk on the phone. IMS. I don't have anything to say. Seeing you was weird.

Mom revs up the vacuum in the hall. I shout his number into the speakerphone. "Come on, man. I know I'm a jerk." She peeks into my room. "Did you say something?"

"No, Mom. I'm on the phone."

She smiles. "Tell Harry I said hello." He says nothing.

"I know what I said to you was awful."

"Right." We breathe together, out of sync. No words.

"I'm sorry, so sorry, really, don't hang up."

He hangs up.

Five minutes later, Mrs. Lassiter tells me Harry is doing homework. "How are you, Frank? Tell your mom I'll definitely see her next week." I listen to her breathe. "Frank, please call another time." She sighs. "I'm sorry."

Generous me, I give him an hour. I hear his mother bark, "It's Frank. Take it."

Harry's voice sounds dull. "I don't know, man," he says. "Maybe someday, but not right now. Right now, I'm still feeling strange. Not pissed. Just uncomfortable. Like you're going to set me up. You . . . you just can't do that, say what you said to me, and expect me to run back when you say okay, I'm cool, I'm ready to act like a human being. I feel for you. I'm sorry for you. But I'm still . . . I'm . . ." We sit quietly on either end of our phone lines. "I've got a date with Joss tonight. Maybe I'll call you later. But, honestly Frank, maybe not."

My e-mail stays empty. I check it every hour, every half hour, every ten minutes. He will change his mind. He always does. He is my best friend.

My e-mail stays empty.

Mom uses every opportunity to drop hints about talking at the high school. If I mention an audiobook, she tells me I can order it from the school library. If I ask her to cook something special, she tells me she'd be happy to make it for a young man who faces his fears.

"Stop it, Mom. I'm not sure I can do it."

"You have to go back sometime," she says. Hint, hint. "It would be nice to show everyone how great you're doing." Hint, hint.

"It's too hard," I tell her. Ten times a day. "I'm not going to let them use me like that."

Dad comes home for dinner three nights in a row. "It would be an honorable thing to do."

The way he looks at me, I almost believe he knows what honor means.

Just before midnight, a message appears:

Harrycarry: Someone at school sent me this:

Frank Marder was recently seen entering Valley Medical Center. Word is that they are looking for improvements in his body, and are hoping for future research possibilities. Look for Frank Marder to speak at many local high schools, including ours. Word is out that Valley Medical is starting a safety awareness project and that they have asked Frank to participate.

I'm glad, Frank. This would be good.

Harry is glad. My parents are hopeful. Stacey is enthusiastic. It would be the honorable thing to do. I motor to my window. It is finally snowing, tiny flakes, the kind that stick to the grass but not to the trees, swirling in the wind.

I sit at the podium of an auditorium filled with students. I hear shouts: *Murderer! Crip! Drunk! Loser!* I try to talk but no one will listen. Someone yells, "Faker!" He begins a chant: *Walk, walk, walk, walk.* I cannot get up. I cannot speak. The auditorium is too loud. *Walk, walk, walk, walk.*

I sit at the podium of an auditorium. No one is there. No one wants to hear what I have to say.

I sit at the podium of an auditorium. Naked. My parents are there. So is Harry. Everyone in the room points and laughs.

I sit at the podium of an auditorium. One person in the back raises his hands. It is Anonymous. He stands, arms above his head, the whole time staring at me. He walks through the silent crowd and joins me on the podium.

"Frank Marder is a sinner," he tells the crowd. "A killer." The crowd cheers. They throw things at my head. I start to speak, but Anonymous covers my mouth. "You have no right." The crowd yells louder.

"Your bed is soaked." Mom strokes my forehead until my breath is normal.

"It's four in the morning," Dad says. They heave me into the chair so she can change my sheets.

Dad wipes my face with a cool sponge. "You had a bad dream." He takes the sheets from my mother. "Here, Rose, let me help."

He steps to the plate.

My mother moves back and watches him smooth the sheets three times with large, strong hands. Then together, they transfer me easily from the chair and into the clean sheets and blankets.

In the morning, I'll call Stacey and say yes.

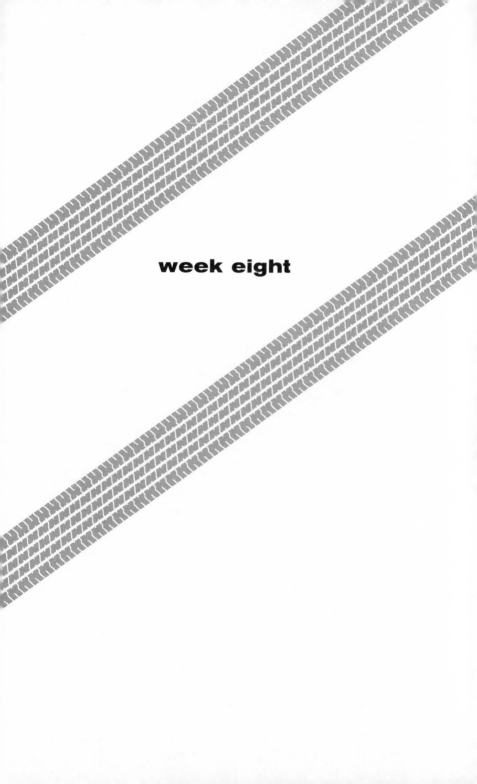

week eight

Mom does not stop dusting until every surface reflects. She restacks the bookshelf. She vacuums twice. She makes a fresh pot of coffee and arranges a plate of cookies in the center of the kitchen table.

"I am so proud of you," she says, plugging in the lemon-scented room deodorizer. She does not talk about God. She does not say, "I love you."

"Let me know when the fumes clear."

A vase of fresh flowers sits on my nightstand. My computer screen is dust-free. "Check e-mail," I command. An empty inbox appears. The doorbell chimes.

"Frank? Are you decent?" as if I could possibly be doing anything illicit. Mom stares at the empty screen; her breath is hot on my neck. Did she think I had an active e-social life? *Hey, baby, yes, you in that sexy wheelchair.*

"It's been a while since I got my last death threat."

She doesn't know I'm joking.

"Stacey's here." Okay, she does know, but I'm not funny.

I say, "Shut down," and motor to the living room. Dad is in the middle of showing Stacey the pictures. Mom turns off the TV. They exchange formalities: How are you, I'm fine, and you? Yes, thank you. Isn't the weather just dreadful? Mom takes Stacey's jacket, and Dad fiddles with the TV guide. The game is starting soon. Stacey better not take all day.

We form a tight circle. "Before we begin, I just want you to know how pleased I am that you have chosen to participate." Stacey puts on her best professional smile. They smile back. All three of them look at me and nod. I look back and grimace. She smoothes out her clingy pink tracksuit and opens a large notebook onto her lap. Around her neck is a thick silver necklace with a dangling heart.

"Dr. Rockingham was sure you would do it. You were our first choice. He knew you would be perfect."

Meredith had a similar necklace, only hers wasn't so shiny. "My aunt Anne gave it to me for my Bat Mitzvah," Meredith had said. "Pain in the ass to polish."

Stacey turns around and rifles through a big canvas tote bag and pulls out a stack of papers. Freeberg was right. Nice butt.

"Would you like a soda?" Dad asks. She nods and he practically runs to fetch three cans of Diet Coke. "You want some lemon?" he yells from the kitchen.

Stacey pulls back a loose strand of hair. "Thanks." She sniffs the air. "I love lemon."

When Dad returns, she picks up her riff. "Let me tell you what will happen." She sips the Diet Coke. Dad sits at my side, back straight, head up, excited and ready to go for the first time in a very long time. "I will speak first. The principal will introduce me and I'll talk about spinal cord and head injuries." She waves four pages of neurology, physiology, and psychology in my face.

Dad scans the packet. "That's interesting, very interesting. Comprehensive."

Mom puts her copy on my tray table. Technical, yes. And precise. Excellent, for a journal article. "It's long." Stacey has clearly never spoken in an assembly at George Washington High. Nobody's going to listen to this.

"Too long?" she asks.

"Yes. A little long." This is a freak show, baby. They are coming for me, the main event. She takes a pen out of her purse. "Maybe you should stick to the most important facts." I suggest massive cuts. She scratches out a few paragraphs at a time until we're down to one page.

She scans what's left, then dumps it in her bag. "After I'm done, I'll introduce you."

Mom gets up and retrieves the plate of cookies, plus some cheese and my favorite snack, a hunk of plain chocolate. She's got straws and little napkins and about a dozen of her oatmeal cookies. When did she bake those?

"Dig in," she says. Dad grabs a cookie, crosses his legs.

"You need to be prepared," Stacey says. "Most of the people in the audience have never seen a person with quadriplegia before."

"Do you have a plan to deal with hecklers?" Mom asks. "You've seen the papers."

"We will only take pre-approved questions. The teachers will collect them ahead of time on index cards. We don't want to deal with any surprises." She covers her mouth and coughs. "You're very brave to do this, Frank."

"They can ask anything they want." I mean it. They want to hear about my pathetic life, who am I to stop them?

The phone rings, and both my parents get up. Stacey stuffs a corner of one of the cookies in my mouth. It takes me at least a minute to chew the thing. The whole time, she keeps talking, faster than earlier. "I am so excited about the project. Next month, if this takes off, *Physical Therapy* is going to do an article about spinal cord injury prevention. Maybe I'll get an interview." She squeals. "I have this fantasy about being on *The Morning Show*."

"That's great," Dad says, back in his place. He eats three more cookies, one after the other. Like drinks.

Mom comes back; she stands next to me and rubs my head in a continuous circular motion. "Do you really think it is smart to start at George Washington? Frank hasn't been back since the accident. There's still a lot of talk."

Stacey nods. "Absolutely. Sunset and I debated starting someplace else, but you have to remember, GW is a magnet high school. We have to go there. We want maximum impact."

"But wouldn't it be better to *start* somewhere else?" Mom is insistent. She stops rubbing. Dad eats another cookie. "Where they don't know him? Where they didn't know Meredith?" She looks to my father. "Will it be safe?"

"Of course it will. But if it makes you feel better, I'll talk to the principal." Stacey jots some notes in her book. "We ultimately decided that it was more important to reach as many people as possible, while we had the funding." She turns to me. "Face it, Frank, wherever we go this year, people will know who you are. They'll know about Meredith." She waits for me to protest, but I don't.

Let them use me.

They finish the snacks. "Frank, I know you haven't been home long, but it isn't too soon to start thinking about your future. Your life. Maybe not now, but soon—sooner than you think—you're going to get antsy." My father looks like a bobble-head doll sitting on the dashboard of a drag racer. "Pretty soon, Frank, you are going to want to start thinking about what you want to do with your life. College. You might even want to get out and have some fun."

I laugh. Yeah, right. Fun. That's a good one.

Meredith said, "You think *fun* is the new f-word."

I shook my head. Not true. "I love having fun." She got off the couch and zipped up her sweater. I pulled her back close. "But Halloween parties are not fun. I told you. I'm not into false faces."

"Everyone will be there." I reached for her hand, but she pushed me away.

"Not everyone," I said. "Not me."

Meredith got up and stood by the window, somehow ignoring my continuous stream of passionate subliminal messages. She peeled off the little ghost from the corner of the pane, shifted it one inch, and patted it back down. She turned her body away from me. She ran her fingers through her hair. Made me feel weak.

She was used to getting what she wanted.

"You don't have to try that hard," I said, getting up and grabbing her, bringing her back to the couch. But I thought, Sit down. Watch the game. Do what I want to do, for once. Just once. She smelled like flowers.

The Steelers were playing the Patriots. Third and six. Two time-outs. Forty-five seconds left in the game. I draped my arm around her. Tight. Flowers, soap, and mint.

"Fine," she said, letting her body go limp. "Don't go. Don't go to the party. I'll go alone. No biggie." Her words were casual, but her tone was fire. She was mad.

She squirmed away and grabbed her coat. The Steelers were driving; the quarterback was stepping back, he was in the pocket. *Come on, defense! Hold them. Or go to a commercial. My girlfriend is pissed.* Football, girlfriend, football . . . Meredith was waiting. She wanted me to apologize. She lingered at the door; she was giving me a chance. I got up and grabbed her, twirled her around. "Okay, I'll go." She walked back into the living room, and we sat down together. Pass. Score.

Success.

"Time to get up." Sunset arrives early to bathe and dress me. "Up for a scalp massage?" she asks. Oh yeah. Give it to me, baby!

She hums and rinses, lets the warm water flow over my ears and scalp and face. I can't help moaning; it feels that good.

"Please don't cut it," Sunset says. "Ever." She massages conditioner into my overgrown curls. "A lot of people with spinal cord injuries shave their heads to make hygiene easier. But your hair is so incredible."

She sighs. I sigh. *Don't stop. Please, don't stop.*

My real clothes—a shirt that buttons, a tie, and a jacket—make Mom start to cry. "Can I take one picture?" she asks. The first time since the accident.

"No. No pictures in the chair." No mementoes.

Sunset begs. "Come on, for my album." She puts her arm around me and smiles at Mom. Sunset can be such a crip chick.

Mom smiles. "It's a day worth documenting." She turns off my battery. *Click.* The last time she took my picture, Meredith was alive. *Click.* We were on our way to the party.

"Smile, Frank."

We walked into the party hand in hand, fingers inside fingers. Meredith was dressed as an '80s diva, complete with black bra, platinum-blond wig, micromini, three wide belts, and pink tights. I wore my father's old Army dress uniform. Mom had found it in the closet and let me have it, if and only if I promised not to tell or spill.

I really, honestly wanted to have a good time. My best foot was forward.

We waved hello, put down our coats in a pile on the couch, and walked into the kitchen, separate, together, separate, together—I held her hand, I lost her hand. She sped up, two steps in front of me; our arms now extended, connected only by two fingers, then one. I held on tight. She tried to squirm away. Tug of war.

"What's the rush, Meri?" I pulled her close. She broke away, waving, walking faster into the crowd, finally free. What was the use? I grabbed a beer and sat on the big couch in the living room. Downed it. Fast. Slammed the empty onto the table, but no one heard. No one saw me without her.

She danced with her friends in a tight circle. No boys allowed. I drained another, maybe a third. She loved to dance. She was having fun. The beer went down easy.

When a good slow song came on, I stood up and tapped her on the shoulder. "Didn't you make this CD?" Stupid comment. I was ready to do anything to keep her.

"Yes," she said, letting me touch her, putting her hands on the edges of my hips. I pushed my tongue in her mouth. My girl-friend. "Frank," she complained. Before the song was over, when all around us people were kissing, she let go.

"See you in a bit." Her voice was tense. Her eyes nowhere near mine. I watched her maneuver her way through the crowd and stop to talk to Paul Rogers. Somehow he was permitted to wear a football jersey and sweats.

Harry came to my side. "Why doesn't she want to hang out

with me tonight?" I asked. Jocelyn looked away. I crossed my arms over my chest. Meredith kissed Paul's cheek. She held his hand. She did not let go.

Jocelyn whispered something in Harry's ear. "We should get out of here," Jocelyn said. "It's too noisy here. Let's go to my house and talk."

Meredith wiggled by, handed me another beer. I grabbed her arm.

"We're leaving."

"I want to stay."

"Are you mad?"

"I just want to stay. God, Frank, why can't you relax?"

Paul tapped her on the shoulder. "Are you having a problem, Meredith?"

She shook her head. No. No problem. Together, they walked to the opposite corner. Music blared.

Harry put his arm on my shoulder. "Sorry," he said.

"Come on, Frank, let's go," Jocelyn said. "Hang out with us. She's acting like a jerk. Talk to her tomorrow. When you're not upset."

I shook them off. Meredith was still my girlfriend. I came to this stupid party for her. We were supposed to be here together.

Another beer. A walk around the house. I found them in one of the back rooms. "Meredith," I said. "I have to talk to you." She didn't look happy about it. She followed me to a quiet space.

"What do you want?" Her eyes looked like they could cut glass.

"If you want to break up with me—"

"Frank." I didn't know what that meant.

"I love you." An outright lie, but the only thing I could come up with. She faced me and sighed.

"Let's go for a drive," she said. "Now. Let's go."

Stacey's agenda is clear ten seconds into her talk. "I have patients who were injured in cars, motorcycles, and snowmobiles. Some of them were wearing seat belts; most of them were not." Her voice shakes. "If you wear a helmet, you improve your chance for survival and quality of life. If you drive drunk, take risks, you can end up with a closed head or spinal cord injury." A few people get up and leave. Stacey speeds up. "Every muscle in your body is connected to your brain through your spinal cord." She dims the lights and begins a PowerPoint presentation. From backstage, I watch. Interesting. If it weren't me.

"Frank Marder was a student here until he was in a tragic motor-vehicle accident. In that accident, he suffered a high-level complete spinal cord injury." She points to the giant spine on the screen. "He was injured here. A little bit higher, and he would need a respirator to breathe. He would propel his chair using a device we call sip and puff." She flashes a picture of some guy moving his chair with a straw. "A little bit lower, and he could bend his elbows, turn his wrists, maybe even make a grip." Sigh. So close. Another slide. "Frank cannot move his arms or legs. He cannot feel anything below his neck. He cannot walk." The lights come on. "Please welcome Frank Marder."

Simon says, everybody clap your hands. Simon says, everybody touch your nose. Simon says, everyone stand up and gawk at Frank Marder, the head case, who cannot do any of the things you just did.

I motor onto the stage. The room turns completely silent, as the boys and girls who take their bodies for granted stare at one of their own, the boy who royally fucked up, the boy who is a head. Master of manipulation, Stacey is. From one corner, I hear, "Shit." From another, "Oh my god. Look at him." The microphones, stationed around the auditorium, pick up every desperate comment.

Breathe. My notes are on the podium. Breathe. The room is full; everyone is looking. Mrs. Gallagher, my fourth-grade teacher, is sitting in the second row. Breathe. There are other familiar faces. Friends of my parents. I look up and down the aisles. Mom. Dad. The principal. Two seats over is Father Joseph. He waves, but I pretend not to see. Behind him is Dr. Rockingham. Jocelyn sits in the corner, an empty chair at her right. I'm not sure why I'm surprised.

Stacey positions the microphone next to my lips. Sweat forms on my neck and drips to never-never land. Two girls in the front row cry. I can't do anything but breathe.

The sea of people waits. Friends of Meredith's—people from class—people I never knew. They are here. Witnesses.

Stacey stands next to me. "You can do it," she whispers. "Talk."

Crash. The side doors open. Too hard. They hit the wall. Everybody looks, but the woman does not acknowledge the attention. She does not lean into the wall, the way all the other late arrivers did. Instead, she struts to a solitary spot in an open space on the right side of the auditorium and stops cold, alone, without support. She is wearing a long coat and a hat with a wide brim. Not appropriate wear for the inside of school, in the middle of the day, when the sun is starting to warm the sky. For a moment, she takes off her sunglasses and catches my eye. She wipes them with her sleeve and puts them back on. Not an effective disguise anyway.

It is Mrs. Stein, Meredith's mom. Ruth Stein.

She may not be on display, but she is as alone as I am. A strange couple, we are, each in our separate space, each with our own pain. No one embraces her—maybe they don't recognize her, maybe they're afraid. She stands, hands in her pockets, eyes fixed on me. She might have a gun. She could shoot me, and if she did, no one would blame her. In fact, maybe someone should tell her that she has a clean shot. *Come on, Ruth, he can't even get out of the way. Do it for Meredith.*

Stacey brings a can of Orangina to my lips. "You need to say something," she whispers. "Now."

Crash. The old man crosses the street.

Crash. Meredith flies through my window.

Crash. Ruth Stein waits for me to speak.

"What's the difference between a . . ." My voice echoes in the hall. "What's the difference between a . . ." Stacey shoots me a worried look. "What's the . . ." She doesn't know where I'm going.

I stop and stare. The hall is completely silent. Every student at George Washington High School waits for me to speak.

"No one said anything."

"What?" Stacey whispers, confused.

"No one said, 'Don't drive.' No one said, 'You've had too much.'"

Actually, no one even said good-bye. We marched to the car, drunk and angry and confused. I swallowed the last beer as we walked out the door—chucked the bottle into the bushes. The "I love you" was a mistake. It didn't chill her out. She was not happy, not fine. But I didn't care. She was leaving with me. Not him.

In the car, she said nothing. Not "Two hands on the wheel," the way my mother does when my father drives after two or three. Not "How could you?" or even "We have to talk." She didn't break up with me, she didn't yell. She stayed slumped against the passenger door until we had left the neighborhood.

Then she turned on the radio and opened the sunroof. She undid her seat belt and lifted herself up, up, up. She ripped off her blond wig and let her long hair whip in the wind.

"Get back in the car," I said, my head still full of alcohol and loud music.

She laughed. "I thought you wanted to have fun, Frank." She raised her hands in the air, laughing, determined to be happy for that moment, so beautiful when she was smiling, when she was having fun, when she was laughing, even when she wasn't really having any fun, when she was making herself laugh and act wild, just trying to make the best of what was bound to be a difficult moment. Pretending that everything was fine.

I was thinking about her and her hair and Paul and the dancing. I kept glancing at her—not the road, not even as we pulled into town. I wanted her to keep laughing with me. Me. Not him. Me—

That's all I remember.

I never saw the man, oh the man, where did that man come from?

I killed her on a simple drive from a party I didn't want to go to.

"I don't know what might have happened if we had stayed."
The collective sigh is audible from the stage. "There was no good reason why any of this happened. We were not bad people. I had a few beers." Five, to be exact. Five beers. One, two, three, four, five.

My script is full of examples and stories of challenges and hardships. Lunch at Mike's. Eating. Getting into bed. Moving in the house. My injury. My problems.

But now that I'm up here, I want to talk about her.

"I killed two human beings. An older man. His name was Lawrence Kitzmiller. And our classmate and friend, Meredith Stein. Dead. Every day, I wake up knowing I killed them. And I am like this." Silence. "There are days when I think they are the lucky ones. Many days I wish I was dead. Every day, I wish I could take it all back."

Stacey stands next to me. "You don't have to do this," she whispers. She points to my papers. "Talk about yourself."

"How do you sleep at night?" someone shouts.

"She was one of the nicest people I knew."

The room buzzes. Meredith had a great sense of humor. Meredith was nice to everyone. Meredith was so full of life. For a few minutes, Meredith Stein is a saint.

No one tells me that I should be in jail. Those words are for anonymous places like e-mail lists and Web logs. No one will lynch me in public.

"Talk about yourself," Stacey whispers. "They need to see you."

"I cannot bathe myself, shave, or drive. I cannot get up out of this chair into bed without the help of my mother and father. Take a piss? Forget it. I cannot do anything but sit and think and talk." I'm on a roll. "Try eating lunch without hands. Try doing anything without hands or feet or even your trunk. My computer is voice-activated. I use a motorized wheelchair that I control with my chin."

Out of air, I cough and gasp. Stacey whispers, "You're talking too fast." She gives me a sip of water. "Take your time. Take a breath."

The audience waits.

"She didn't deserve to die."

A girl shouts out, "You should have called a cab."

"Yes. I should have called a cab."

Other students speak. "Only beer? You only had beer?"

They ask about Meredith. "Did she say anything? Did she know she was going to die? What do you remember? Was she in pain?" The questions I ask myself each day. I don't know if she knew. No, I can't remember. I hope she felt no pain.

They ask about the car, the beer, the emotion. The costumes, the dark night, the winding roads, slippery when wet. The way we think—we think we're invincible. Yes, yes, yes. All those things are true. Remember the rules.

When I drove my car over that old man, into that tree; when Meredith Stein flew out of the car, onto the sidewalk; when my neck broke, *snap*, in two, none of my prior good acts mattered. In school, we learn about Newton's Laws of Motion. If you are not pushed, you will continue in one direction, at one speed. An object's velocity will only change if a force is placed on it. For every action, there is an equal and opposite reaction. We are told to believe that. I believed that.

"I never thought something like this could happen to someone like me."

When I am done, some stray people stand and clap. Most file out of the auditorium, talking quietly. Resuming their lives. Stacey may think she got to them, but by the time Saturday night rolls around, the beer will flow. No one will remember to be careful. She cannot prevent the next me.

As the room empties, Ruth Stein remains. She watches the kids walk by, one by one. The adults congregate in small circles; she is the only person besides me who doesn't move.

Finally, when there are only a few stragglers left in the room, she takes very small steps toward the stage, and hands something to my mother. The two women are almost exactly the same height. Ruth Stein speaks, and Rosemary Marder nods. She does not talk back. They do not embrace. They turn together and look at me, but they do not move toward the stage.

"I am really proud of you, today, Frank." Stacey organizes her papers; I remain at the podium. My notes sit unread. No one stops to talk to me. No one congratulates me.

My parents shake hands like celebrities. The principal embraces my mother. This is not what they had in mind last September when they envisioned me at the podium addressing the students. But today, they smile.

A bell rings. My parents push me back to the car and take me home, no words necessary. Stacey follows in her bright yellow Jeep. She stays for lunch. Chili with cheese and sour cream. Meat, cheese, and pepper in every bite.

"We have two school visits next week, then one every week after that for the next two months."

"You did a good job." She looks proud.

My parents look eager.

When Stacey leaves, they remain at the table. My mother reaches into her purse and retrieves a small piece of paper. She unfolds it and holds it at eye level. "This is for you."

It is a letter. My name is written at the top of page.

"It's from Meredith's mother, isn't it?"

Her face is expressionless. "Yes, it's from Ruth Stein."

"Have you read it?"

Mom shakes her head. "I told her I wouldn't."

"Hold it up to my face."

Her writing is small and precise, a combination of cursive and block. Square, not loopy. Upright, not slanted. A lot like Meredith's handwriting.

"Frank, you did a great thing today. Thank you. From Anonymous."

Anonymous. Yes, of course.

Ruth Stein, the mother of the girl who died, the only person who has the right to hate me, is my supporter. Anonymous.

For the first time in a long time, I laugh. I really laugh. It doesn't start out strong, but it is real and so I laugh harder. My mother looks startled. Delighted. She covers her mouth. My father's eyebrows arch. He smiles, too.

Yes. It makes sense. I read the words again and let my laugh tumble. It feels good to laugh. Yes. I *feel* it. A real laugh, not hearty, not sarcastic, not condescending, but joyous, thankful. I laugh. My ears ring. I can laugh.

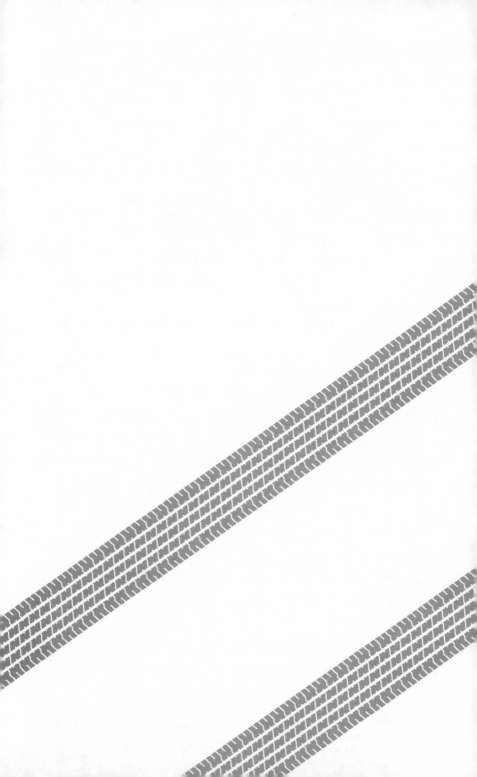

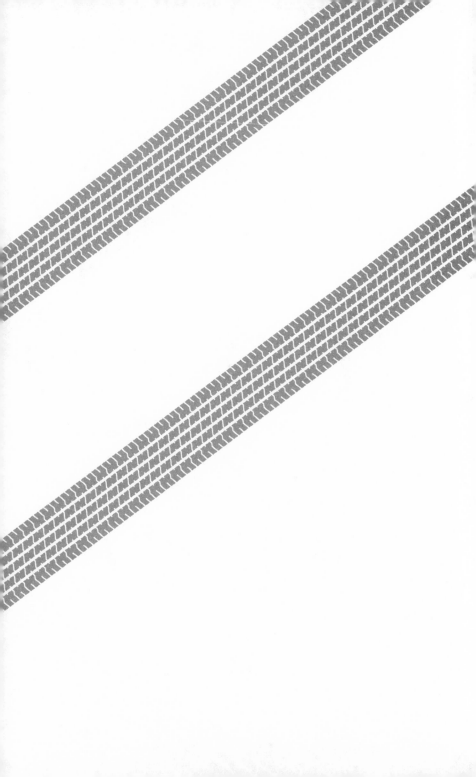

about the author

Sarah Aronson says, "When I was in physical therapy school, we were asked to spend some time in a wheelchair. We had to maneuver up ramps, into bathrooms, and through crowded halls. It was almost impossible. Luckily, when we were tired, we could simply stand up. We could walk away. We were just fooling around.

"I have always admired the sheer will of people following a traumatic injury. As a physical therapist, I worked with many people to overcome obstacles and return to society. But I rarely saw them after discharge. I often wondered what life was like outside the rehab unit.

"That said, in writing Head Case, I never set out to show people what it is like to sustain a spinal cord injury. I wanted to explore a character who felt trapped and labeled, a character who needed to rise above society's judgments, forgive himself, and move beyond his mistakes."

Sarah Aronson lives in Hanover, New Hampshire, with her family. This is her first book.

Library Media Center
NEUQUA VALLEY HIGH SCHOOL
2360 95th STREET
NAPERVILLE, ILLINOIS 60564

Neuqua Valley High School

FIC ARO
Aronson, Sarah.   Head case

3004000151537N